# KAEL

*Texas Rascals Book Six*

# LORI WILDE

K ael Carmody was back, and everybody in Rascal, Texas, knew the minute he breezed into town. His name set off sparks from Mildred's Diner to the all-night Laundromat on First Street to Dorothy's Curl-Up-and-Dye.

Nothing in Rascal had changed in the seven years he'd been away. Kael still set matrons' tongues wagging and young women's hearts swooning.

Everyone except Daisy Hightower.

Daisy was twenty-six. She was also independent, hardworking, and as stubborn as Kurt McNally's old mule. She could also carry a grudge longer than anyone in the Trans-Pecos.

Kael found that out the hard way.

But he had other things on his mind besides Daisy when he strolled into Kelly's Bar off Highway 17, looking for liquid refreshment and an order of Kelly's famous chicken-fried steak.

"I don't believe my eyes," Joe Kelly exclaimed, resting a bar towel on his shoulder and extending a palm. "Kael Carmody, as I live and breathe."

Taking care to minimize his limp, Kael hitched himself up to the red vinyl bar stool, doffed his straw Stetson, and clasped

Joe's hearty handshake. Back in high school, he and Joe had played on the Rascal baseball team together.

"How's the leg?" Joe asked, casting a glance downward.

"Healin'."

Kael wasn't ready to talk about the accident or his shaky prognosis. The less said, the better. But avoiding the topic in Rascal posed a real challenge. Thankfully, the tavern was empty at one thirty in the afternoon, except for the two guys shooting pool in the corner, and Kael didn't know either of them.

"You gonna be able to ride again?" Concern knotted Joe's mouth.

"Sure." Kael pulled a confident face that was complete bluster. "Just home recouping for a few months."

"Gotta be tough." Joe nodded.

"Yeah. How 'bout a longneck and an order of chicken-fried steak? I'm starved for your cooking. There's nothing like it."

Joe beamed at the compliment and pulled a beer from the ice. Twisting the top off, he slid the bottle across the bar to Kael. "I'll go start your order."

Kael swiveled on the bar stool, sipping his beer. He swung his gaze around the bar. There was still a tear in the screen door. The same posters hung on the rough-hewn, shiplap walls. An oscillating fan rotated at the back of the bar. The windows were open, bringing in the scent of high desert, sand, and long-buried memories.

Memories he'd rather forget. Memories that had kept him away from Rascal for so long. Memories of Daisy and their lost love.

If he closed his eyes, he could still see her firm, tanned figure in that purple bikini, still smell the coconut aroma of her sunscreen, still taste the frosty Italian ices they'd shared at Balmorhea Springs in the summers.

Dang!

Why was he thinking about that hardheaded creature? He'd

2

gotten over her years ago. Just because he'd come back home to recover didn't mean he was entertaining any ideas about getting together with her for old times' sake.

Knowing Daisy, if he dared show up on her front porch, she'd tell him to scat before she sicced the cops on him. Who needed that kind of grief?

"Here we go," Joe said, proudly sliding a plate of chicken-fried steak with mashed potatoes and cream gravy in front of Kael. "Bet you haven't had steak this good since you left Rascal."

"You'd bet right." Kael dug into the food.

"Hmm," Joe said. "Just you wait. I'm having a blow-out barbecue at my place for the Rodeo Days celebration in June, and you're invited. Not just invited, but as the most famous person from Rascal, you're the guest of honor."

"I'm not that famous."

"The heck you're not." Joe snorted. "How many people have made it to the Professional Bull Riders Championship in Las Vegas three straight years in a row?"

And, Kael wondered, how many of those people got so badly wounded doing it, they lost their careers or even their lives?

"Only folks who follow rodeo have ever heard of me," Kael said. "Besides, that and five dollars will buy you one of those fancy coffees at Starbucks."

"Like you have to worry about money." Joe shook his head. "You're the only child of the wealthiest family in town. You're destined to inherit a two-thousand-acre cattle ranch. What's the problem?"

Kael didn't know what would happen if his leg didn't heal. Three different specialists had come to the same conclusion. Slim chance he'd ever ride again without a radical new surgery. But it was no panacea. Even though his manager, Randy Howard, was pushing the operation, Kael hesitated.

If something went wrong, he might never walk without a limp.

Kael winced. What was he going to do? Bull riding was his life, his identity since he was twelve years old. Sure, he could follow in his father's footsteps and become a rancher, but Kael possessed such a strong case of wanderlust that he couldn't envision himself settling down any place. Especially in a dried-up, go-nowhere town like Rascal.

His nomadic nature was what killed things between him and Daisy. Kael winced and ran a palm along his jaw.

One of the pool players sauntered over to the old Wurlitzer, and Dolly Parton's voice filled the room.

Kael finished his food and pushed the platter across the bar. "So how *are* things in Rascal?"

"Your folks don't keep you up to date?"

"They spend most of their time in San Antonio these days and leave the running of the ranch to the foreman, so they miss out on the local gossip."

"Well." Joe steepled his fingers. "The drought's been rough on everyone."

"I saw."

On the drive in, he'd noticed parched pastures, scrawny cows, and the dried-up stock ponds. Rascal was in the high desert of the Davis Mountains, so there wasn't ever lush greenery, but he couldn't recall ever seeing the place this barren.

Luckily, his parents divested their holdings and could weather a few lean years, but that wasn't true of everyone in Presidio County.

"A few farmers have gone bankrupt."

Kael clicked his tongue. "I hate hearing that."

"Cattle prices are the lowest they've been in sixteen years."

"That's what my dad's been telling me." Kael knew about the drought and the farmers' problems. What he hungered for were details on the townspeople...and one special person in particular.

"Guess who I saw yesterday?" Joe asked as if reading his thoughts.

Kael shook his head and took another swallow of beer. The outside of the bottle was sweaty. The coolness already dissipating in the heat. "Who?"

"Daisy Hightower."

His heart stilled, but he kept a nonchalant expression on his face. "Yeah?"

"She's just as fine as she was in high school. Maybe more so." Joe swiped a damp towel across the counter.

"Good for her. She always was a beautiful woman."

"Waste if you ask me."

"What's a waste?" Kael quirked an eyebrow. Despite his best intentions, he couldn't deny the curiosity zipping through him. He'd love to see Daisy again. Question was, would she love to see him?

"The girl never dates. Stays home, works those beehives, and looks after her sister's boy. She's turned into a regular hermit."

"Rose has a child?" Startled, Kael frowned.

"Had."

"Had? What?"

"Rose is no longer with us."

"You mean Rose is dead?"

Joe nodded solemnly.

Jolted, the news hit Kael like a slap, and he almost choked on the swallow of beer he'd just taken. Why didn't he know this? "What happened?"

Joe made a face. "She abandoned the boy right after he was born. Left him for Daisy to raise. Then two years ago, Rose overdosed on sleeping pills in some New Orleans flophouse. Real sad."

5

"No kidding?" An icy blast chased down Kael's spine, and he regretted eating the greasy food. The news left him shaky.

"You remember how wild that girl was, partying nonstop, a different boyfriend for every night of the week. I'll admit it. I kept company with her a time or two myself. Who didn't?"

*I wish I hadn't,* Kael thought, the old self-loathing returning with a vengeance.

"Daisy's had a hard time."

"I imagine she has, raising a kid on her own," Kael mused.

"Uh-huh. She legally adopted Travis."

"Nobody could accuse Daisy of slacking." Kael peeled the label off his beer bottle. And avoided Joe's eye.

"You ain't got no interest in rekindling old flames?" Joe settled his elbows on the bar and leaned forward to cup his chin in his palms.

"With that fiery redhead? You gotta be kiddin'. I'd just as soon stick my hand in one of her beehives. It'd be a lot less painful." Kael snorted, but inside dormant feelings stirred. Feelings he didn't care to examine too closely.

"Want another beer?"

"Nah." Kael shook his head. "I better be getting home. Mom's cooking up a big dinner tonight and inviting all the relatives over." Truthfully, he'd heard enough gossip for one afternoon.

"Don't be a stranger," Joe said, "anytime you wanna talk rodeo, you got an audience."

"Thanks."

He didn't need a reminder of that, either. Why torture himself? Until he decided one way or the other about the surgery, he didn't want to discuss bull riding. Kael could just see himself whiling away the days, hanging out in Kelly's Bar and gabbing about what used to be or what might have been.

Daisy Hightower and bull riding. The two things he'd loved

most. The same two things that had caused him the greatest heartache in life.

Snagging his Stetson off the bar, Kael dusted the brim, then settled it on his head. He took money from his pocket, but Joe held up a palm.

"This one's on me, good buddy."

"Come on, Joe, take the cash." Kael pushed the twenty at him.

"You tryin' to insult me?"

"All right, have it your way."

Kael folded the twenty and stuck it back in his pocket. He wasn't about to let Joe get away with this. They'd been friends since high school, and although Joe earned a fair living running the bar, he had a wife and three kids to support. The guy just might wake up one morning to find a new freezer sitting on his front porch waiting to take the place of the one wheezing in the back room.

"You oughta go see the woman," Joe said as Kael reached the door.

Kael turned to look at his friend. "Who?"

"Daisy. You never know. She might have changed her mind about you."

"Are we talking about the same Daisy?"

"Motherhood has mellowed her."

"Like it mellows grizzly bears?" Kael lifted his shoulders. "No, thanks."

"Your call."

"Yeah." Kael stepped out into the oppressive heat.

Honey bees floated near the horsemint outside the door. Not a single tree stirred, and heat mirages shimmered up off the asphalt. Absentmindedly, he rubbed his aching leg and crossed the parking lot to his pickup truck.

Those danged bees brought back a lot of memories. Memories of clear spring mornings and sweet amber honey. Memories of colorful flowers and buzzing hives. Memories of stealing honey-sweetened kisses from Daisy Anne Hightower.

"Forget her," Kael muttered, slamming his truck into reverse and backing out of Joe's parking lot. "You got enough problems to contend with. What's over is over, and Daisy will never be yours again."

Shifting into drive, he bit down on his lip and reeled from the hardest slap of loneliness he'd felt in seven years.

❧

"Did you see Kael Carmody?"

"Oh my gosh, hasn't he got a body to die for?"

"And those eyes of his, so mesmerizing."

"I was too busy scoping out his backside to pay much attention to his eyes."

Overhearing the checkout girls' conversation, Daisy's hand froze around the jar of pimentos she was about to drop into her shopping cart. Her pulse gathered speed, and her legs went wobbly. She took a deep breath to steady herself.

*Please, Lord,* she prayed. *Say it isn't so. Tell me Kael Carmody isn't back in Rascal.*

"Do you think he'd go out with me?" one girl asked. She was a plump blonde, who wore her hair pulled back off her face. The girl wasn't much over nineteen.

The same age Daisy had been when Kael had broken her heart and shattered her world.

"Don't be silly, Deedee. You are way too young for him. Besides, Kael could have his pick of any woman in Rascal," the other young woman, a willowy brunette, replied.

*Not me!* Daisy thought, straining to eavesdrop. *Not if he were the last man on earth.*

She'd learned the hard way there should be much more to a man than good looks and a penchant for fun. And if her own lessons hadn't been enough, all she needed to do was remember Rose and *her* mistakes.

"Still." The one named Deedee sighed. "He's too fine for words. Sorta puts me in mind of Scott Eastwood."

"Everybody puts you in mind of Scott Eastwood," her friend teased.

"You can hardly tell he limps."

"They say his bull riding career is over."

"Guess that's why he's back home."

"I hope he pops in here often. It'll make work a lot more exciting."

Kael's career at an end? Daisy's mouth twitched as mixed emotions rocketed through her. She would love to say she was over Kael, but she couldn't lie to herself. She harbored tender feelings for the man, despite what had happened between them, and she cursed herself for that weakness.

She knew how upset he'd be if he could never ride in the rodeo again. Daisy had heard about Kael's accident. Even someone as much of a recluse as she could not have missed hearing about that.

Kael's tragic spill at the PRC in Las Vegas had been big news, overshadowed only by the Dallas Cowboys' Super Bowl run. But Daisy didn't know Kael's injury had been so serious, and that news grieved her.

Worry knots formed in her stomach. How many times had she experienced the same roller-coaster sensation while watching Kael tear out of the chute on the back of some wild Brahma? She'd washed her hands of him seven years ago and good riddance. But she couldn't stop the ache that gnawed at her.

Angry with herself, Daisy tossed her head and maneuvered her grocery cart down the produce aisle, safely distancing herself from the checkers and their discussion of the man who'd been a thorn in her side for far too long.

Why did she care if he'd gotten hurt? If he was still dumb enough at his age to keep climbing up on those bulls, then Kael deserved everything he got.

*Kael's back.*

That irritating thought echoed in her mind, refusing to leave no matter how hard Daisy willed it away.

Why couldn't she stop wondering what he looked like now and how well he'd weathered the years? Those same seven years that had been the most trying years of Daisy's life. Years spent struggling to raise Travis, dealing with the aftermath of her identical twin sister's death, and trying desperately to forget that Kael ever existed.

*Get your head back on your business and finish your errands*, she scolded herself. Hurriedly, she completed her shopping and stood in line for Deedee to check her groceries.

She paged through social media on her phone while she waited, trying to distract herself from thoughts of Kael. She wondered how come he hadn't returned to Rascal before now and what brought him back home this time.

After paying for her purchases, Daisy wheeled her cart to the parking lot and loaded the groceries into Aunt Peavy's Jeep Wagoneer.

Her aunt Peavy had come to live at Hightower Honey Farm after her parents died in a car accident when she and Rose were sixteen. Her sister had never accepted their parents' deaths.

Daisy believed that Rose's inability to move forward caused her wild, reckless behavior…and ultimately her tragic overdose.

She sighed. No point fretting about something she couldn't change. The past was past, and she had to keep looking to the future, for Travis' sake if not her own.

At the thought of her adopted son, Daisy's heart swelled with love. He'd be getting out of school any minute, and Daisy was never late picking him up. Her only regret in taking care of her nephew was that she had no time for dating.

And if she couldn't date, how could she find a husband? And if she couldn't find a husband, how could she hope to have more children?

Wistfulness filled her. How badly she wanted a baby of her own! She couldn't love Travis any more if he'd come from her womb, but Daisy longed for the experience herself. She wanted to be pregnant, to live through the joys and challenges of bringing a child into the world.

But she didn't want to do it without the right man by her side. A man of good moral character. A man who would be there when she needed him. A responsible man who would put his family first.

A man the exact opposite of Kael Carmody.

🐍  2  🐉

**D**aisy guided the Wagoneer down Presidio Boulevard.

She pulled to a stop at the red light, and the vehicle clattered.

*It's nothing,* she assured herself. It had to be nothing, she could not afford car problems right now.

A powder-blue pickup sporting a lot of shiny chrome pulled up behind her, the engine idling smoothly.

Daisy glanced in the rearview mirror, wanting a truck like that. It boasted a wide bed, just perfect for hauling farm equipment. Glossy running boards and flashy floodlights mounted on an overhead roll bar.

*Like you could make those payments.*

The pickup probably belonged to some drugstore cowboy who'd never stepped foot on a real ranch in his life.

She squinted. The driver wore a straw cowboy hat and sunglasses, but with the tinted windows reflecting the sun's glare back in her eyes, she couldn't tell much else about the man.

The light turned green.

Daisy eased her foot off the brake and pressed on the accelerator. The engine surged, but the Jeep refused to slip into gear.

Oh, no! Daisy groaned. *Not the transmission.*

Her neighbor, Keegan Winslow, had been warning her about the sound of Aunt Peavy's transmission for a month. They'd put off having it looked at because they could not spare the minimum two grand it would cost to have the car repaired.

*What now?*

Praying for divine intervention, Daisy tried again, but the old Wagoneer only squealed and didn't budge.

She sighed and lowered her window, motioning for the pickup to go around.

The driver didn't move.

Daisy motioned again.

He stayed right behind her.

"Suit yourself," she muttered. She had enough concerns without worrying about this guy, like how to get to the elementary school within the next five minutes.

The pickup's emergency flashers came on, and the driver's side door opened.

Great. A hero to the rescue. Daisy rolled her eyes.

"Let him help you," she muttered, fighting her natural tendencies. She had inherited the infamous Hightower stubbornness, and she found it hard to accept help. But in this case, she better swallow her pride.

Watching through the rearview mirror, she saw one jean-clad leg appear, then the other. This guy moved as slow as Christmas.

Brushing her hand through her hair and forcing a smile, Daisy got out and turned to greet the stranger. The apology froze on her lips.

There, sauntering straight toward her, was Kael Carmody.

Her heart stuttered.

A familiar grin cocked the corners of his full mouth. The

straw Stetson riding high on his forehead gave her a good view of his thick thatch of whiskey-brown hair. His large hands rested loosely at his narrow hips. With mirrored sunglasses and a huge, gold rodeo belt buckle glinting in the sunlight, he looked cucumber cool.

A dozen different emotions swept over her, and she didn't want to feel any of them.

Daisy caught her breath at the fierceness stabbing her chest. Many times, she'd envisioned their chance meeting. She'd imagined herself calm, aloof, unimpressed. She had practiced the lines she would speak, the moves she would make. She'd dress to the nines, her hair perfectly coifed, her nails painted and buffed.

Instead, she wore her usual attire—ratty work jeans, a simple white T-shirt and battered work boots. She had pulled her hair back into a ponytail with a rubber band, and she wore no makeup. Her cuticles were ragged, and her fingernails unpolished.

But worst of all, she had this almost irresistible urge to fling herself into his arms.

"Hello, Daisy." The words rolled off his tongue soft and easy.

"Kael." She nodded, struggling to keep her self-control while her knees wobbled.

"Don't I even get a hug after seven years?" He held out his arms.

"Considering the circumstances around the last time we saw each other, I don't think you deserve one."

"I thought maybe you'd forgiven me by now."

"In a pig's eye."

He dropped his arms to his side. "Same old Daisy."

Her heart tripped. "Nothing changes here in Rascal. I recall you once told me that before you took off."

"Dang. But you're a fine sight for sore eyes."

Was it a flight of her fancy, or was his voice thick?

*If he sounds emotional, it's probably because he stopped off at Kelly's Bar for a beer, not because he's feeling anything for you.*

"You're more beautiful than ever," he murmured.

"Cut the soft-soap, Kael. I'm not a gullible nineteen-year-old anymore." Her heart thudded so loudly she feared he could hear it pounding from two feet away.

He pursed his lips but said nothing.

The sun beat down, scorching her scalp. Uncomfortable, Daisy transferred her weight from one leg to the other and folded her arms over her chest.

"Aunt Peavy's green monster giving you trouble?" he asked, switching his gaze to the stalled Wagoneer.

"Transmission."

Kael slipped off his sunglasses and dangled them from the stem.

Daisy raised her chin.

Their eyes met.

Something inside her shifted. The hard, cold knot of pain and betrayal that had taken root in her heart seven years ago billowed against her rib cage, resurrecting the old hurt. She thought she'd buried her feelings for this man long ago. Obviously, she was wrong.

Kael dropped his gaze. Leaning over, he peered into the Jeep's back seat at the brown paper sacks mingling with her beekeeping supplies. "Have you been grocery shopping?"

"Yes."

Reminding herself of all the trouble Kael had caused, Daisy narrowed her eyes and pressed her lips together in a firm, unyielding line. She could not, *would not*, let him see he still affected her like no man on earth.

A car whizzed around them, the driver honking his horn.

"We need to get you out of the road," Kael said matter-of-factly, folding his sunglasses and sliding them into the front pocket of his light-blue Western shirt. The shirt looked brand-new, as did his sharply creased blue jeans and those fancy ostrich boots.

"Don't trouble yourself," she said. "I can manage."

"Daisy, don't be stubborn." He reached out a hand to her, but she shied away.

She longed to tell him to get lost, to go soak his head, to darn well make like a cow patty and hit the trail, but school was out, and Travis would be waiting.

"Okay," she agreed.

A wide grin sprawled across Kael's face as if he'd just stayed eight seconds on the back of the meanest Brahma on the rodeo circuit.

"I'll push you off to the side, then we'll call a wrecker."

She nodded. There was no money for a wrecker, but what else could she do? Climbing inside the Wagoneer, she waited while Kael ambled back to his truck.

*He's trying hard not to limp*, she noticed, surprised at the surge of sympathy arrowing through her. She did not want to feel sorry for Kael. He had chosen his lifestyle. He'd known the consequences when he'd climbed on that bull.

Daisy gulped against her unwanted sympathy and blinked back the tears that threatened. After all this time, why did she still feel the urge to weep when she thought about what they'd both lost?

Kael eased his pickup forward. She felt the gentle tap as metal bumped metal. Steering the Wagoneer into the shallow ditch, she pulled it off the road.

Hands clenched into fists, she waited while he walked back to her vehicle. Without another word, he opened the tailgate and scooped three grocery sacks into his arms.

His masculine scent—a combination of spicy cologne, musky hay, and fresh clean sunshine—filled the car.

The aroma slapped Daisy with a blast from the past. Memories of long summer days and cool summer nights. Memories of wet kisses and warm embraces. Memories of their mouths joined as they traded heady pleasures.

Enough!

Daisy shook her head, grabbed the two remaining sacks, and trailed behind Kael. The past was past. There could be no going back.

Kael took the paper bags from her and fitted them into his extended cab before walking around and opening the passenger-side door for her.

"Where to?" he asked.

"I've got to pick up my son, Travis, at school."

*That ought to throw him for a loop. Let him wonder where she got a child.*

But to her surprise, Kael merely nodded and got behind the wheel. "Clinton Elementary?"

"Yes."

"What grade's he in?"

"Finishing first."

"Hard to believe that you have a child that old."

*He could be your son.*

Daisy slid a glance in Kael's direction. Over the past seven years she'd studied her son's face many times, trying to find a resemblance to some man in Rascal. Her greatest fear was that she'd discover similarities between the boy and Kael. But Travis had taken after the Hightowers with his rich auburn hair and fair, freckled skin. If he had any feature that matched Kael's, it was his hazel eyes.

If Kael was Travis' father, she didn't know what she would do. Even after Rose left town, Daisy had not risked calling Kael and telling him he might be a father. What was the point?

She'd known he wasn't responsible enough to be a real dad. He'd refused to give up his rodeo career for her. Why would a baby be any different?

*Let sleeping dogs lie.* That was her motto.

Daisy stared straight ahead, noticing the bug guts on the windshield. Anything to keep from looking at Kael Carmody. Why did he have to be the one to drive up behind her when the green monster had picked that moment to die?

"What do you want to do about the Wagoneer?" Kael eased his truck through the twenty-mile-per-hour school zone.

"I don't know." Trying her best to stave off a headache, Daisy lifted a hand to her temple and rubbed.

"Do you need money to have it towed?" he asked.

"No!" Daisy barked. She'd crawl through the mud, on her hands and knees, before she would accept money from Kael. She darted a quick glance in his direction.

Kael snorted and shook his head.

"What's that mean?"

"Haven't changed, have you? Still too danged stubborn to let anyone help."

"I don't need help," she denied hotly.

"Suit yourself."

Daisy raised her eyebrows, surprised that he hadn't argued further. That was different. In the past Kael would have insisted until their push-pull of wills dissolved into a shouting match.

He came to a stop outside the elementary school. Dozens of children skipped across the lawn, freed from another day of learning. Daisy's eyes searched the throng for Travis.

She spotted him, sitting off by himself, gazing dreamily at the sky. He looked so small, so vulnerable. Many times, she'd wondered how a woman as wild and impetuous as Rose had produced such a quiet, introspective child. Was Travis' biological father introverted? If so, she could allay her fears that Kael had a hand in the boy's conception. Kael was not the shy, retiring type.

Rolling down the window, Daisy stuck her head out and waved. "Travis, honey, over here."

The boy looked up, and a smile broke across his face. "Mom!"

He gathered up his books and ran toward the pickup. Daisy opened the door and scooted over for Travis to climb in beside her.

❧

KAEL STUDIED THE THIN, YOUNG BOY WITH THE SERIOUS EXPRESSION on his slender face. "Hi."

Travis ducked his head.

"Say hello," Daisy prodded.

"Hello," Travis murmured. "I like your truck."

"Why, thank you, Travis." Kael extended his hand across the cab, and he accidentally grazed Daisy's shoulder.

The contact sent white-hot sparks sizzling down his nerve endings. Gulping, Kael kept his gaze focused on the boy, and he wondered if Daisy had also felt the earth tremble. "My name's Kael."

Travis shook his hand and offered Kael a shy grin. "Nice to meet you, Mr. Kael."

"No mister, just Kael."

Daisy had done a fine job raising him. It couldn't have been easy, playing both mother and father to her sister's child. *You and Daisy could have a baby of your own by now.*

The thought, like a lonely phantom, passed through his mind. His sadness intensified, and he felt a sudden and deep regret for his life choices.

They drove down the street. Silence, like an accusation, hung between them.

"How's the beekeeping business?" Kael asked.

"All right."

"I thought maybe the harsh winter might have caused you some trouble."

"We lost a lot of bees," Travis said solemnly.

"Really." Kael frowned. "I'm sorry to hear that."

"But we're doing fine," Daisy insisted.

Was Hightower Honey Farm in financial trouble?

"If you need any money..." Kael made the offer even though he knew he risked riling Daisy.

She gave him a sharp look, and Kael read her thoughts. *Not in front of Travis.*

At one time they'd shared an uncanny telepathy, as if their minds traveled the same track. Apparently, the ability still existed. Kael pursed his lips and stared out the window.

"What do you want to do about the Wagoneer?" he asked again, turning onto Presidio Boulevard.

Daisy stared down at her hands, and Kael realized she had no money for a wrecker or car repairs. Dang the stubborn woman. If she'd allow him, he would take care of everything. But being essentially on her own since sixteen had made Daisy used to standing on her own two feet. She didn't take handouts, especially from him.

Travis raised his head and stared at the Wagoneer in the shallow ditch. "What happened to the green monster, Mom?"

"Transmission went out," Daisy mumbled, "but let me worry about the car."

Kael pulled over on the shoulder, engine idling. "Do we haul it to the shop now, or do you want me to take you home?"

She rubbed her temple with her fingers. "Would you take us home? I need time to sort things out before I decide what to do."

"You got it."

Kael knew how much effort it took for her to make that simple request. He also knew that he would have the car towed and the repairs made behind her back and let the chips fall where they may.

He drove out of town, headed toward Hightower Farm. How many times had he driven this road with Daisy beside him? A melancholy sensation tightened his chest, and he sneaked a glance in her direction.

She was staring out the window, her hands resting in her lap, her chin held high.

She was more beautiful than he remembered, with that long, red hair glowing in the sunlight, her peaches-and-cream complexion bronzed to perfection, her full lips pursed into a determined pout.

Man alive, but he wanted to pull the truck over, drag her out the passenger-side door, and kiss her until she begged him to come back into her life.

But Kael knew that would never happen. Daisy was a woman of strong convictions. It was one thing he admired most about her. Once she decided on an issue, she didn't change her mind.

And seven years ago, she'd ended their relationship.

Kael had cloaked his pain by focusing on bull riding. He'd lived and breathed rodeo. There had been no other lady to steal his heart since Daisy.

Oh sure, he'd dated casually, but he'd let no one get close enough to burn him the way Daisy had. A man could only take so much suffering before he turned his back on love.

And then a bull had taken away his ability to ride. He'd lost that love, too, just as surely as he'd lost Daisy.

He felt a hot, hard sensation inside him—regret, remorse, sadness, sorrow. Guiding the pickup toward Hightower Honey Farm, Kael yearned for a second chance.

He killed the engine. More memories swept through him as his gaze drifted over the farm.

The house begged for a fresh coat of paint, and the fence needed stretching. Grass grew ankle-deep. Overgrown tree limbs hung low. The place fairly cried out for a handyman.

*At least she hasn't found someone to replace me.* Startled at the direction his mind had taken, Kael shook his head.

He recalled sitting right there on that same front porch swing with Daisy. They had kissed and giggled and held one another until Aunt Peavy came out on the porch with a pitcher of fresh-squeezed lemonade and a tray of chocolate chip cookies.

He'd once helped Daisy and Aunt Peavy in the apiary. They'd united colonies, cleaned the hives, clipped the queens. A humming noise rose in his memory along with the sweet aroma of honey.

Yes. Hightower Honey Farm brought back a lot of old feelings. Feelings he couldn't recapture. But maybe, just maybe, Daisy would allow him to be her friend. He hated to think he'd lost her from his life forever.

"Hey, Travis, why don't you carry this sack inside for your mother?" Kael reached into the extended cab and handed the boy a small sack of groceries.

Travis nodded, took the sack, and climbed to the ground.

Daisy followed him, but Kael laid a restraining hand on her shoulder. "Wait. I'd like to talk to you alone."

She hesitated, wariness in her eyes. "What do you want?"

Kael swallowed. "The farm needs work, Daisy."

"I'm doing my best," she snapped. "You think it's easy? Running a business and raising a six-year-old?"

"That's not what I meant. I'm very aware of how hard you work."

"Then what did you mean?" Daisy's green-eyed gaze had a hard edge to it.

"You could use a man around here."

One eyebrow shot up high on her forehead. "Oh, no, Carmody, you're not about to weasel yourself back into my life."

"There you go, jumping to conclusions. I can see you're still the same old Daisy." Irritation snapped through Kael. He'd forgotten just how hardheaded this flame-haired woman could be. "I have absolutely no intentions of pursuing you."

Daisy folded her arms over her chest.

Irritation transformed into something darker, deeper. Memories. Swallowing his angry words, Kael met her stare.

Daisy didn't even blink. She leaned over the seat and pulled out grocery sacks and set them on the ground outside his truck.

"I'll get those." He opened the door and walked around the pickup.

"I can unload my own groceries."

She was one tough cookie. He had to give her that. But even the hardest of cookies crumbled under the right conditions.

"I want to help. Let me pay for having the green monster repaired."

"No way. It's not your problem."

"Daisy, I care." He reached out a hand to touch her, but she shook him off.

"You don't owe me anything, Kael."

"I was hoping to be your friend," he whispered, realizing that was true. If he couldn't have her as his girlfriend, then he'd settle for anything to be near her.

"You and I could never be just friends, Kael." She slammed the pickup door, and the sound echoed the finality of her statement.

"Daisy."

"Please," she said, her eyes filling with pain, and it killed him because he knew that he was the reason for her suffering. "Do us both a favor and stay out of my life."

**❧ 3 ❧**

**D**aisy's chest hurt, and tears burned her eyes. Clutching two grocery sacks, she stumbled into the house.

"Mom?" Travis looked up from the kitchen table where he was eating a peanut butter and jelly sandwich.

"Daisy?" Aunt Peavy wiped her plump hands on her apron then adjusted her thick glasses and peered at Daisy.

"I'm fine." She gritted her teeth. Resting the sacks on the table, she spun on her heels and marched back outside for another load.

Thankfully, Kael's pickup was halfway down the road, leaving a dust cloud in its wake. The setting sun glinted off the shiny chrome, announcing to the world at large that Kael had returned home to Rascal.

Her bottom lip trembled. *Don't you dare cry. Haven't you shed enough tears over that man?*

Swiping her hand under her nose to ward off the waterworks, she hefted the remaining sacks and trotted back inside.

"Are my poor old eyes deceiving me, or did I spy Kael in our driveway?"

"It was Kael," Daisy confirmed with a sigh.

There was no mistaking the delight on her aunt's wrinkled face. "Well, why didn't you invite him inside, dear?"

"Auntie, I don't want Kael getting any ideas."

"That history is water under the bridge. No reason you and he can't be friends."

Oh, there was a great reason all right. It hurt too much to even sit next to him in the pickup cab much less see the man regularly.

Daisy didn't respond. Instead, she stacked groceries into the pantry.

"I guess he came home to recover from that knee injury," Aunt Peavy mused.

"I guess so," Daisy muttered.

"He has a cool belt buckle," Travis chimed in. "It's gold and huge and has a picture of a cowboy riding a bull."

"Kael's a famous rodeo bull rider," Aunt Peavy told him.

The boy's eyes widened. "Really? Wow."

Daisy didn't like the way her son's face lit up over Kael.

"Yes, and he got hurt badly climbing up on those bulls," Daisy said.

"I wish I could watch him." Travis chewed his sandwich, a dab of purple jelly smeared across his cheekbone.

"Kael's bull riding days are over." The wistful feeling wafted through Daisy surprised her. Even though Kael's career had torn them apart, she knew how much the rodeo had meant to him. She could only guess at how awful he must feel, cut off from the thing he loved most.

Darn it, why did she have to live next door to the man?

Running a hand through her hair, she hoped Kael wouldn't be staying in Rascal for long. Surely his wanderlust would soon take over and he'd leave.

Just as he had seven years ago. Except this time there was no dream to chase.

"Daisy?"

She blinked and stared at Aunt Peavy. "Beg your pardon? I wasn't listening."

"What are we going to do about the green monster?'

"I don't know."

She rubbed her throbbing temple again. Her responsibilities were never ending—always a crisis to handle, finances to fret over, a figurative fire to put out.

The past winter, she'd battled a bad bout of foulbrood that infected the apiary. She'd lost hundreds of thousands of bees in that outbreak. Also, the recent drought had decreased the number of flowering plants and affected honey quality. Her colonies were the weakest they'd ever been. Recouping her losses would take over a year or more.

"How will Travis get to school in the morning?" Aunt Peavy asked.

"He'll take the bus, and I'll see if Keegan can give me a tow to Willie's garage," she said, referring to the neighbor that bordered the back of the property.

"I've got a little money stashed away," Aunt Peavy offered. "It's not much, but it'll help pay for repairs."

"But that's your Christmas money," Daisy protested.

"It's only May. I'll have plenty of time to save more cash for Christmas."

Daisy mulled over the idea. She hated taking money from her aunt, but right now she had little choice. They had to have a vehicle and borrowing from Aunt Peavy was preferable to accepting help from Kael.

DOWN IN THE DUMPS JUST ABOUT COVERED THE WAY KAEL WAS feeling. Seeing Daisy again yesterday afternoon had done nothing to ease his unhappiness. In fact, it was painfully obvious he'd made a bad choice seven years ago. He'd picked bull riding over love, and now he had neither and a bum leg to boot.

His parents were throwing a party in his honor, and he wanted nothing more than to escape. He remembered now why he hadn't come back to Rascal before. The memories were just too painful. Over the years he would either visit his parents at their condo on Padre Island or they saw him on the rodeo circuit.

Until the accident, he'd had no desire to return home. Glancing over his shoulder at the rambling ranch house where he'd grown up, Kael hitched in a heavy sigh.

Music blared from the windows. Dozens of cars parked in the driveway and around the side of the house. The smell of barbecue lingered in the air, but he wasn't hungry.

No one seemed to notice he'd slipped away from his own welcome home party. After fielding a million questions about his injury and his failed career, he'd tolerated as much autograph signing and backslapping as he could muster, then he'd mumbled something about getting fresh air, grabbed a beer from the cooler, and disappeared outside.

He went to the barn and stripped the protective tarp off his motorcycle. The vehicle looked as fresh and new as the day he'd bought it. One of the ranch hands fired it up periodically and performed the minimum maintenance required.

He'd purchased the Harley with money from his first PBR win.

Dang! He wanted to ride the powerful motorcycle, to feel the hard metal between his legs, the wind rushing through his hair, the engine vibrating throughout his body. Yet another experience the accident had robbed from him.

Except it hadn't been an accident. He'd willingly climbed upon that wild Brahma. Had proudly strutted his way to the chute.

He had risked his health, his future, for the glory of the

moment. At the time, he hadn't regretted it. Back here in Rascal with Daisy still nursing a grudge right next door, Kael held a whole new respect for regret.

But there was nothing he could do to change the past, and right this minute, he wanted to ride that Harley so badly he could taste it. Kael tilted his head and eyed the motorcycle. What could it hurt? A ten-minute run through the pasture.

His leg throbbed like a son of a gun, but he didn't care.

What did he have to lose? Jutting out his chin, Kael walked the motorcycle from the barn. His hands caressed the glossy finish, and he straddled the seat.

*You could make your leg worse.*

The thought floated through his mind, but he pushed it aside. How could things possibly be worse?

Heck, he should live it up while he had a chance. He'd discovered the hard way that life was far too short, and that nothing, but nothing, could remain the same.

The rebellious streak that had been a part of him since childhood egged Kael on. It was that wild streak that had driven him to seek his fortune riding bulls. The same streak that had prodded him to make a name for himself and prove to the world he was more than Chet Carmody's pampered son.

Desperate to blur the hurt stirred up by Daisy's rejection, Kael kick-started the motorcycle and ignored the pain shooting up his leg.

A familiar thrill rumbled through him. A thrill he hadn't experienced since New Year's Day when the Texas Tornado had tromped him into the arena dirt.

Kael gunned the machine and started off across the dry pasture.

Even though it was early May, the drought had already taken a toll on the withered grassland. Long stalks that should have been bright green were parched yellow instead. Grasshoppers leaped from beneath his tires as he blasted across the field. The sun beat down, hot and relentless.

Sweat trickled down the hollow of Kael's throat. Grass slapped against his thighs. His left knee ached, but he ignored the discomfort. He wanted to ride fast enough to eradicate Daisy from his mind.

Increasing his speed, Kael traveled along the fence line dividing his parents' property from Daisy's. The smell of honey mingled with the scent of white clover and alfalfa.

He roared through the alfalfa field, stirring up honey bees as he went. His parents had been watering the crop, otherwise Daisy's bees would have had little to feed upon.

Daisy's bees.

Kael briefly shut his eyes and swallowed. He saw her standing before him, covered in bees, a smile on her face, honeycomb dripping from her hand. She'd been sixteen to his eighteen, and she had smitten him.

She'd been so brave, so fearless. Just like he was on a bull's back. It was only later that she taught him the secret that allowed her to stick her hand into the hive without being stung.

He'd never known another woman like her.

Not before, not since.

Daisy was one of a kind. She accepted no excuses, made no allowances for herself or anyone else. When her parents died, she'd taken over running the honey farm without a misstep. She harnessed herself to hard work and responsibility like a horse to a plow.

Exactly his opposite. Responsibility had always seemed like a prison to Kael. He recalled the words Daisy had hurled at him during their last fight. She'd called him a coward. Had she been right?

He'd told himself he was pursuing his dream, making his mark on the world and accepting the wanderlust that gripped him. Had he been running from commitment? Had his love for

Daisy been so strong he feared the power and used bull riding as an excuse to escape the intensity of his feelings?

*Stop thinking about the past.*

Kael gunned the motorcycle, revving the engine higher, faster, until the alfalfa flashed before him, a yellow blur.

The sun scorched his skin, the ground, the air.

Sparks flew from the exhaust.

Bees circled, irritated by his maneuvering.

Kael swung the Harley in a wide circle and made another pass through the alfalfa. Perspiration coated his whole body, and he reveled in the sensation. Dirt, sweat, dust, speed. It reminded him of the rodeo.

A white cloud rose from the fodder field.

Kael narrowed his eyes and frowned. *What the heck?*

Smoke.

No mistaking the odor.

The cloud billowed and spiraled, spreading quickly throughout the tall hay.

Panic, hard and sudden, slammed into Kael's stomach.

Sparks from the exhaust must have caught the pasture on fire! Stunned, he pulled his Harley to a stop, idled the engine, and watched.

The air filled with frantic bees, diving, swarming, buzzing in a thousand directions desperate to escape the fire, but smoke dulled them.

Daisy's bees! They couldn't take prolonged exposure to the intense heat. His heart dropped.

Bright orange flames licked at the alfalfa, rising higher.

Kael stared in horror as the bees struggled to keep flying then, bunch by bunch, tumbled headlong from the sky.

Oh, Lord, what had he done?

"DO YOU SMELL SOMETHING?" AUNT PEAVY ASKED, HER NOSE twitching as she sniffed the air.

"No." Daisy studied the ledger spread out before her. She was sitting on the back porch, taking advantage of the noonday shade offered by the awning, while Aunt Peavy watered her flowers.

Taking a sip of fresh-squeezed lemonade, Daisy frowned at the book. Unfortunately, figures didn't lie. Hightower Honey Farm was in serious financial straits.

If they scrimped and saved and nothing unforeseen happened, they could survive this disastrous season. But just barely.

By winter, if she were very careful, she might have enough money to purchase a few new bee colonies.

"I definitely smell smoke," Aunt Peavy insisted. "The Lord might have given me poor eyesight, but he made up for it by blessing me with a strong sniffer. Take a deep whiff, Daisy. It's not my imagination."

To humor her aunt, Daisy laid down her ledger and inhaled deeply. "Auntie, I don't—" She stopped short.

Hmm, there was an acrid scent in the air. It wasn't surprising if something had caught fire considering the prolonged drought and the relentless heat.

"You think somebody's burning trash?"

"Surely not. There's been a county burn ban on for three weeks."

Aunt Peavy paused to switch off the water hose. "It's close," she whispered. "Real close."

Daisy dropped the ledger and sprang to her feet. Shading her eyes with her hand, she scanned the horizon.

There. South. Toward the Carmody ranch. A smoke column chugged skyward.

Aunt Peavy was right. The fire was close. Right in the Carmodys' alfalfa field which bordered her apiary. The bees

31

loved pollinating the sweet fodder. This time of day, the bees would be out collecting nectar.

Sudden fear flooded her body, bathing Daisy in a cold sweat.

Not the bees!

Her knees swayed. No. She couldn't panic. Clenching her jaw, she started across the yard, her legs churning as she ran.

*Please God, don't let the bees get hurt.*

A fire engine wailed in the distance. Her pulse galloped, and her eyes glued to the sky. She saw a heavy swarm converge high above the alfalfa field.

*Fly home, fly home,* she silently urged, but in her heart, she knew it was too late. The bees were too near the heat.

The closer she got, the thicker the smoke grew. Daisy coughed, tasting exhaust fumes. Her side ached, and her eyes burned.

The swarm appeared shaky. They weaved and dipped as if they were having difficulty flying.

Anxiety had her biting down on her knuckles. This could not be happening!

The fire engines drew closer, the plaintive wail growing louder, stressing Daisy's anguish.

She reached the fence separating her property from the Carmodys' place. Gripping the fence post in both hands, Daisy stared at the fire crackling just three hundred yards away.

The blaze licked hungrily at the alfalfa stalks, progressing steadily northward toward her land and her beloved bees.

Helplessly, she watched as her bees tried to form swarms but got caught in the heated updrafts. They circled sluggishly then disappeared into the thickening smoke.

*No, no, no!*

It doomed her bees, and she knew it. Daisy moaned and clasped her hands to her ears, trying hard to deny the carnage occurring before her eyes.

Her nose burned. Her throat felt raw and swollen. She coughed and blinked.

A figure emerged from the smoke. A man. Beating the flames with a blanket. Daisy squinted and coughed again.

Kael.

Daisy crawled over the fence. Ducking her head, she edged closer to the inferno. Heat waves shimmered in front of her face. The fire snapped and rustled. The air exploded with the odor of burning alfalfa.

"Daisy!" Kael shouted.

She looked up.

"Go back." He waved her away. His face was red and covered in soot.

"It's useless." She reached out and grabbed his shirt, pulling him backward. "Stop before you get hurt."

A grim expression marred his handsome features, and Daisy suppressed the urge to hug him. Why did she have this crazy desire to comfort him?

Kael would lose nothing more than alfalfa harvest. And with his money, that was a drop in the bucket, whereas she had lost her bees and her entire livelihood.

He tugged away. "I've got to put out the fire. It's killing your bees."

"Too late," she replied.

Sweat mingled with the soot on his face, streaking his cheek black. He clutched the battered horse blanket in one hand and stared desolately at the widening area of destruction.

"I'm so sorry," he whispered.

"It's not your fault," she soothed.

"Kael! Daisy!"

Shouts drew their attention behind them. A mob of people, including Kael's parents, ran toward them. A quarter of a mile away, the volunteer fire truck turned into the Carmodys' driveway.

The wind changed and blew smoke into their faces. Daisy coughed continuously.

"Come on, let's get back." Kael took her elbow and propelled her toward the gathering crowd several feet behind them.

She leaned against his chest, and he brushed the hair from her face. She blinked and peered at the people surrounding them.

Daisy labored to draw in a breath. Her bees were dead. Gone just as surely as her mother and father and Rose.

Slipping from Kael's grasp, she slumped to her knees, exhausted. Someone laid a comforting hand on her shoulder, but it didn't ease her sorrow.

The fire trucks bumped across the field. Volunteer firemen scurried like ants, battling the blaze.

Looking up, she saw Kael and his father join the firefighters.

"Here's water." Kael's mother squatted next to Daisy.

Daisy took the proffered water bottle and swallowed thirstily.

Neela Carmody gave her a sympathetic smile. The woman looked as if she'd stepped from a ritzy catalog in her crisp white blouse, white linen pants, and expensive Italian sandals. Kael's mother always wore the most fashionable clothes and never had a hair out of place. She was chic and sophisticated, everything Daisy was not.

"What happened?" she asked.

Swiping her sleeve against her forehead, Daisy pushed her bangs from her eyes and shrugged. "I don't know. Aunt Peavy smelled smoke, and I spotted the fire in your alfalfa field. When I got here, Kael was trying to put it out with a horse blanket."

"Did it get to your bees?" Neela lifted a hand to her mouth.

Daisy nodded. "They're gone."

"Oh, honey. I'm so sorry. I know how important your bees are."

"Thanks," Daisy croaked. What an understatement. The bees were vital to Hightower Honey Farm.

"If there's anything Chet or I can do, please ask."

"Thank you," Daisy said, knowing she'd never ask them for anything.

"I mean, with Kael being home and all..." Neela allowed her words to trail off as if realizing how silly she sounded.

"Everything is over between Kael and me. Has been for a very long time."

"I know that. I thought, well... to tell you the truth, Daisy, I'm worried about his mental health. You know he hasn't been the same since the accident. He's brooding and moody. Not at all like his usual self."

From what Daisy had seen of him yesterday, Kael seemed fine.

"I thought it might be nice if Kael had old friends he could turn to for moral support."

Daisy shook her head. "That's not such a great idea. I'm sure Kael's got plenty of other friends in Rascal."

"I suppose you're right." Neela sighed, stood up, and gazed at the firefighters through her pricey sunglasses.

Daisy felt a little odd, sitting here talking to Kael's mom. Even though they lived next door to each other, she rarely saw the Carmodys. They kept a condo on Padre Island, letting a manager oversee their ranch. They moved in different economic circles, making it unlikely that they would often cross paths.

It hadn't been hard avoiding Kael's parents. Daisy was so busy. Their occasional contact comprised a low-key exchange of pleasantries whenever they met in town. Or a friendly wave when they passed on the road.

The Carmodys were nice folks, and she hated the rift between the two families, but the last thing she wanted was a personal relationship with Kael's family.

Daisy watched glumly as the firemen gradually got the blaze under control. At least it hadn't crossed the fence onto her property. But it really didn't matter. The fire had wiped her bees out.

What was she going to do now?

Glancing at the ground, Daisy spied a bee carcass. Her bottom lip trembled. Reaching down, she scooped up the damaged insect and cradled the poor thing in her palm.

Gulping back the tears burning her eyelids, Daisy stared at the creature that had worked so hard making honey for her.

"Are you all right?" Neela asked.

"Yes," Daisy lied.

It seemed life was always dishing her up a bowl of fertilizer. She wanted to leave, but she didn't have enough energy to get up and go home. Telling Aunt Peavy about the bees would require more strength than she possessed at the moment.

The fire chief, Kael, and Chet walked over to them.

Daisy noticed Kael limped heavily, and her heart lurched.

"I think it's under control, Mrs. Carmody." The ruddy-faced fireman wiped at his face with a cloth.

"Thank you, Jim. We surely appreciate your quick response."

"We do our best." He doffed his hat.

"Yes." Kael clasped the man's hand. "Thank you."

"Got any idea what started this fire?" Jim looked from Kael to his father and back again. "You folks know there's a burn ban on, dontcha?"

"I do," Kael admitted grimly. His jaw clenched as all eyes swung his way. "I caused it."

Daisy stared. Had she heard him correctly? Kael had started the blaze that killed her bees?

"I was riding my motorcycle through the field. Apparently, the exhaust sparked and caught the dry grass."

Trembling, Daisy rose to her feet. She should have known. Here she'd been feeling sorry for him, worrying about his limp and his mental health, while he'd been gallivanting about on a motorcycle, oblivious to the problems he could cause.

"Daisy." He reached out to her, his eyes pleading for forgiveness.

But she shied away, skirting a wide berth around him. "Don't."

"You've got to know I didn't mean for this to happen," he said.

She pressed her lips together in a cold, hard line. "Face facts, Kael, you'll never grow up."

With that she pivoted on her heels and stalked across the burned, smoking alfalfa field, the dead bee's body clutched in her fist.

☙ 4 ☙

Even when he'd lain bleeding in the arena dirt at the PRC championship in Las Vegas, his knee mangled by the Texas Tornado, Kael hadn't felt pain like this.

After chasing the dream for seven years, he'd returned home to put his life back together only to repeat the same mistakes he'd made in the past. He'd let his rebellious nature rule his head.

Forgetting the look of despair on Daisy's face was impossible.

Kael sat on the split-rail fence, raking his gaze over the destruction. The air stunk of burned alfalfa. He could taste the caustic flavor. The whole pasture was black. Hours later, smoke continued to spiral upward in lazy patches.

Daisy had every right to her anger. He'd let her down.

Again.

How different might his life have been if he had given up bull riding for the only woman he'd ever loved?

*But you didn't.*

No. Instead, he'd let the best thing that ever happened to him slip through his fingers in favor of a career with no stability, no longevity, no guarantees. A career that had earned him a ruined leg and a lot of pain.

If he had stayed, he and Daisy would probably have married by now. With two or three children of their own. Daisy wouldn't have to worry about money. They would fill their lives with love and laughter instead of sorrow and loneliness.

Kael cracked his knuckles and recalled the cocky young man he'd once been, so sure of himself. Confident that fame and fortune were the keys to happiness. Convinced that making a name for himself would prove to his successful father, once and for all, that he was a man.

His recklessness had cost his parents an alfalfa field, but that was nothing. His folks had insurance. The toll was much higher for Daisy and her little family.

He had to make amends. If he could just figure out how to approach her.

"Ah, Daisy," he whispered under his breath. "I never meant to hurt you."

Kael glared at the Harley still parked beside the fence. Daisy was right. It was about time he grew up and accepted responsibility. Now if she would only let him.

Determined, Kael eased himself down off the wooden fence and mentally girded himself for task ahead.

"WE'RE RUINED," DAISY WHISPERED.

For once, Aunt Peavy had nothing to say. She sat at the kitchen table looking as shocked as Daisy. Her iron-gray hair, normally well coifed, lay plastered against her head.

Tears left makeup tracks down her plump cheeks. She smelled of the cinnamon buns she'd made for their breakfast that morning, but instead of cheering her, the sweet aroma stirred her sadness.

She clenched her teeth. She could tolerate the pain for herself. But it hurt so badly to see how this turn of events affected her aunt.

"Hightower Honey Farm has been a staple in Presidio County for three generations." Aunt Peavy mopped her face with the tail of her apron. "I'm sorry to live to see this day."

"Now, Auntie." Daisy got up and gave her a hug. "Don't get upset. I'll think of some way to save the business."

"How? Without bees, there is no honey."

"I'll get more bees."

"With what? We're flat broke." Aunt Peavy wrung her hands. "We're gonna end up on the street."

"I'm sorry I let you down." The lump in her throat grew.

"Heaven knows you've done your best, sweetie." Aunt Peavy patted Daisy's arm. "I'm not accusing you. If anybody's to blame, it's that no count rascal Kael."

Part of her agreed, but the kindhearted part of her knew Kael was hurting too. He'd lost his career, and he was at loose ends. He didn't know riding his motorcycle in the alfalfa field would end up causing a fire. He was contrite. She'd seen it in his face.

But she had bigger problems than making Kael Carmody feel better. He was on his own in the self-soothing department.

"There's no use crying over spilled milk. The bees are dead, and we've got to make a fresh start."

"What are we going to tell Travis?" Aunt Peavy fretted.

"The truth."

"The poor little lad." Aunt Peavy sniffled.

"Travis is tough. He'll manage, just like we will."

Daisy put up a brave front, but in her heart, she was as worried and frightened as Aunt Peavy. What *were* they going to do? Where *would* she get the money to pay the bills and buy new bees?

The front doorbell rang.

"I'll get it. You collect yourself." Daisy got to her feet.

Mentally giving herself a shake, Daisy opened the front door.

Kael stood on her porch, head hanging low, his Stetson in his hands.

The sight of him took Daisy's breath. No matter what the man had done, no matter the pain he'd caused her, she still could not seem to stop her heart from tripping over itself.

"What do you want?"

"To make amends."

"Oh, go ride your motorcycle," she said. "It's not up to me to relieve your guilt."

"Daisy, give me a chance."

"Since when did the great Kael assume responsibility for his actions?"

"Since now." He rested his hand against the doorjamb as if to keep her from slamming the door in his face, and he looked her right in the eyes.

She felt as if he'd sucked the essence from her marrow with his blistering gaze. "Yeah, right."

"Will you just hear me out...please?"

She sighed. "What is it?"

"May I come in?"

"All right, but I can't promise Aunt Peavy won't swat you with her broom."

Kael moved ahead of her into the foyer. Daisy closed the door against the insufferable heat and watched him limp toward the living room. She motioned to the couch, and he eased himself down. Daisy sat beside him but put two cushions distance between them.

"I talked to our insurance agent."

Daisy folded her arms across her chest. "Yes?"

"Our policy will cover the loss of your bees."

Swallowing her pride, Daisy nodded. "It's a beginning."

"I know I owe you much more than that. Money might buy

you bees, but I realize there's a lot of work involved in starting new colonies."

"Yes, there is."

"I'll help."

"No way. I don't need you hanging around causing more problems."

"It's the least I can do," he insisted, sliding across the couch toward her.

Daisy leaned back. What was that warning spark in his eyes? "No. Absolutely not."

"You've got more than you can handle, running a business, raising a six-year-old, and taking care of an elderly woman."

"I'm not that old, young man!" Aunt Peavy scolded, shuffling into the living room. "And he's right, Daisy. You've got to have help. Already you get up at five in the morning and don't find your way to bed until almost midnight."

"Auntie," Daisy spoke sharply. "I'll handle this."

"The man wants to make amends. Who are you to deny him?"

The woman whose heart he'd broken those many years ago, that's who. Daisy couldn't bear the thought of Kael constantly underfoot. The thought of Kael running around with his shirt off, doing physical labor, had her contemplating a cold shower.

"Look, if you don't let me help, I will go nuts. You'd be doing me a favor," Kael said.

"Why on earth should I do you a favor?"

"Pity?" He gave her the grin that could melt any female within a hundred-mile radius. "I don't have a thing to do. I'm sitting around at my parents' house, waiting for my leg to heal, binge-watching Netflix and getting fat."

"Don't forget starting fires in your spare time."

Heavens, how she wanted to say yes. But did she dare? This time could she keep her heart from harm's way?

ॐ॒ॐ

KAEL FOLLOWED DAISY ACROSS HER BACK PASTURE TOWARD THE beehives. He couldn't believe she would let him help her. She must be in more pressing financial straits than he first believed. He knew from experience that this hardheaded woman rarely changed her mind about anything.

"I haven't checked the apiary since the fire. Come along. You might as well see the damage you've caused."

Her words added to the guilt already towering inside him.

By the time they'd traveled the short distance to the apiary, sweat plastered his shirt to his back, and his leg thumped with pain, but he refused to give in to it. This was the high desert. He'd dry soon enough.

Daisy stopped short. She placed her hands on her hips and gazed at the dormant hives, eyes widening and bottom lip trembling.

Gone was the normal hive hustle and bustle. A few frantic bees circled, nervous and unsettled; the remaining bees raised their heads from the hive and lined up between the tops of the frames.

Stepping to the work shed, Daisy went inside, then returned with two white veil hats and a bee suit.

"Here," she said, handing him the bee suit. "Put this on. They're upset and more likely to sting."

Nervously, Kael donned the zippered, white coveralls, tugging them on over his clothes. Who normally wore the coveralls? They were far too big for Daisy.

Was there a man in her life?

Jealousy stabbed through him. Joe told him Daisy hadn't been dating, but Joe didn't know *everything* in Rascal. Perhaps she had a secret beau.

"Whose coveralls?" he asked.

"Aunt Peavy's. But she rarely helps with the bees anymore. Her eyesight is too poor."

"Oh." His spirits lifted.

Daisy removed more equipment from the shed. She carried a contraption that resembled bellows and another tool. Settling the bee veil over her head, she crouched and struck a match to light the smoker.

Walking past Kael, she approached the hive, coming at it from the side and taking care to avoid the flight line of the remaining bees.

He watched, fascinated.

She moved with practiced ease. The afternoon sun glinted off her hair, shining like some glorious crown. A deep, abiding ache started in his gut and fled upward.

Daisy Hightower was more beautiful than ever. Her skinny girlish shape had rounded into womanly curves. Her freckles had lightened, and her face had grown to fit those wide green eyes.

He'd been such a silly fool seven years ago. He'd thrown away their budding love affair for bull riding. Then that awful incident with Rose had capped off his sins. Now, by starting the blaze and killing Daisy's bees, he had blown any chance he might have had at rekindling their old flame.

"Pay attention." Daisy turned her head to stare at him. "If you're sincere about helping me rebuild, then you've got to know what's going on. I'm checking on each queen and seeing exactly how many bees I've lost."

"Okay."

Bees gathered around the opening, buzzing angrily. Kael winced and steeled himself.

With the smoker clutched in her right hand and the hive tool in her left, Daisy blew two smoke puffs into the hive entrance.

The smoke calmed the bees.

Daisy removed the hive's outer cover and blew a puff of

smoke into the center of the opening. Taking the hive tool, she pushed it gently into the inner hive.

Realizing he'd been holding his breath, Kael forced himself to suck in the air that smelled of smoke and charred alfalfa. She worked slowly, gently removing each frame and examining hive activity. He watched, fascinated by Daisy, the bees, the whole process.

Sighing, Daisy replaced the frames and then the cover. When she turned to face him, he saw tears glistening in her eyes.

"Daisy?" Alarm raced through him.

"This hive is almost completely wiped out. The queen is okay, which is good. But I've lost at least fifty thousand workers."

"I'm sorry," he whispered.

"I know they're bees and not people." Her bottom lip trembled. "But they meant a lot, you know?"

"I...I..." He had no idea how to respond. Her tears hit him like a solid punch to the solar plexus. He'd caused this—her anguish, her grief, her despair.

"I can't bear to look at the rest. Not now. Maybe later." She stepped away from the hives and stripped the veil from her face.

She wiped at her cheeks with the back of a hand.

He removed his veil and went to her. "Daisy, I can't tell you how I regret what I've done."

Tilting her head, she angled him a green-eyed glance that had Kael thinking crazy, illogical thoughts. How he wished for a time machine where he could return to the past and do things over. If God granted him a second chance with her, he'd do his level best not to fumble again.

The sun shone on her face, accentuating the sprinkle of freckles across the bridge of her nose. Her lips, a lovely shade of peachy rose, lay perilously close to kissing distance. Her complexion was flawless. She didn't look a day older than she had seven years ago. Kael's breath hung in his lungs.

"I've missed you so much," he whispered.

"Have you?" Her pulse thumped at the hollow of her throat.

"So much."

Panic flared in her eyes, and she gulped. "Oh, Kael."

Did she want him as much as he wanted her? Her body language seemed to say so. Her mouth softened, and she was leaning toward him.

Impulse seized him before he had time to consider his actions. Kael took her by the shoulders and tenderly planted his mouth on hers.

The brushing of their lips was pure heaven, sweeter than the most succulent honey. Old feelings roused in him just as powerful as ever. He wanted her. Desperately. And not just physically. Kael wanted something far more meaningful.

Daisy's breath came hot and ragged. Her body tensed beneath his fingers.

"What are you doing?" She jerked away.

"I... I just wanted to comfort you."

"Yeah, because kissing helps me *so* much," she said sarcastically. "Keep your hands off me, Carmody."

Dang! He'd made another terrible miscalculation.

"I'm allowing you to assist me on the farm because I have no choice. But this relationship is strictly business. Got that?"

"Daisy, please. Let me explain." The hardness in her eyes cut him to the quick. "I'm not the same guy you knew seven years ago."

She snorted. "Who are you trying to convince? Me or yourself?"

"I've been doing a lot of thinking since the accident and..."

"There's no atheist in a foxhole."

"What?"

"A bull trampled your leg, and that changed your whole life. Yeah, right. You're just feeling a little mortal right now, Carmody.

You're still the same devil-may-care womanizer you always were."

"I was never a womanizer." Heat burned the tops of his ears. "You've been listening to too much gossip, Daisy Anne. I might have had a reputation for having fun, but that didn't mean I made a habit of one-night stands."

"Right. And that explains why you slept with Rose."

Kael froze. He'd known that eventually they would have to deal with this issue; he just didn't think it would be now.

"I tried to explain to you what happened that night, but you wouldn't listen to me."

Daisy raised her chin. "You expected me to believe you over my sister."

"It was the truth."

Pain zinged through him as the memory slammed into his brain. Over the years, he'd tried to put the image from his mind, but he'd never been able to fully erase it.

Even now acid burned his throat, and his stomach tightened as he recalled the night his life had completely unraveled.

It had been a warm Saturday evening, and he'd just won a PBR rodeo in San Antonio. They held the next event in Oklahoma, and Kael could talk of nothing else.

He remembered the drive back with Daisy in the pickup beside him. He'd been full of glory and excitement, chattering nonstop about his career until he'd realized Daisy was strangely silent.

"What's the matter, honey?" He'd reached across his pickup's seat to take her hand. "You're awfully quiet."

"You'll leave me, won't you?" she'd blurted.

Kael had tried his best to skirt the topic, two-stepping around the truth, but Daisy was no fool.

"Bull riding means more to you than I do."

"No, it doesn't," he'd denied.

"How can we get married if you're off chasing the rodeo

circuit?" She had folded her arms over her chest, shutting him out. It rankled.

"Whoa there. I love you, Daisy Hightower, but we're way too young to get married."

"I didn't mean right now."

"Then there's no rush. Plenty of time for me to have a career."

"Are you sure you just don't prefer the parties and the girls that hang around?"

"Is that it?" Her jealousy flattered him. "You're afraid someone will steal me away? Honey, I love you and nobody else but you. Why don't you come with me? We can follow the circuit together." He'd squeezed her hand, but it hadn't calmed her.

"Kael, I've got a bee farm to run; I can't just walk off. Rose and Aunt Peavy depend on me."

"Well, then, if they're more important to you than I am..." He'd let the sentence dangle.

After that they'd had a big blowout, ending with Daisy issuing an ultimatum, and Kael refusing to give up rodeoing.

Deep in his heart he'd known she hadn't meant it when she'd told him they were through. His plan had been to let her cool off and try to talk sense into her the next day. He'd make her understand that one day, after his rodeo career was over, they would get married.

Despite their fight, he'd still been in the mood to celebrate his victory. He'd dropped her off at home, then made his way to Kelly's Bar.

He wasn't proud of the fact he'd downed too many beers. But he'd been angry at Daisy for spoiling his night.

What happened next was inexcusable—his only defense was that he'd wanted to make love to Daisy so badly he couldn't think straight.

He was drunk. Kael admitted it. When the bar door swung open and Rose walked in wearing one of Daisy's dresses, her hair pulled back in Daisy's signature ponytail, her lips adorned with Daisy's pink lipstick, he'd assumed Rose *was* Daisy.

Rose, playing her role to the hilt, had apologized for arguing with him. She'd kissed him passionately, caressed him, and urged him to take her somewhere private. His good fortune had excited Kael.

For months, he'd dreamed of making love to Daisy, but she'd been holding out for marriage. He'd respected her wishes, but here she offered that most precious gift—her virginity—and begging his forgiveness. Blinded by love and suckered by his hormones.

If he'd been sober, he would never have mistaken Rose for Daisy. Public displays of affection were not Daisy's style. But he'd been so desperate to make up with her, so hungry for her approval, so eager to mend fences he'd followed Rose like an eager puppy.

Even now, Kael's face flamed with shame at the memory.

He and Rose had gone to the ranch. They'd slipped out to the barn. He didn't remember much else. Except that he had called out Daisy's name.

Then suddenly Daisy had been standing in the doorway, looking shocked and hurt as her twin sister made love to her boyfriend.

Kael winced. The ensuing scene had been ugly and full of recrimination. Rose had told Daisy that Kael seduced her. Kael had tried to make Daisy understand that he had confused Rose for her.

But Daisy was having none of it, and how could he blame her? He'd wounded her in the most profound way imaginable.

"I'm really sorry about what happened," Kael said hoarsely, shaking the memory from his head. "It changed the course of my life."

"Mine, too." Daisy's gaze skewered him like beef on a barbecue spit.

"You don't know how many times I agonized over what I did."

"Ah, poor baby." Her words were cold.

"Danged hard living without you. That's why I haven't come back home. It hurt too much."

"You think it was easy for me?" Anger snapped in her green eyes. "Assuming responsibility for Rose's mistake, raising Travis alone, knowing there's a strong possibility he's your son!"

"Wh... what?" Kael stared as the words sunk in. "What do you mean? Travis *can't* be my son."

"Rose discovered she was pregnant only weeks after you slept with her. Did you bother with protection, Kael, or were you too drunk?"

Kael's mouth dropped open, and he stared at Daisy. Shock, more violent than any earthquake, jolted through his body. If someone had shot him in the gut, he wouldn't have been more astonished. Was it true? Could that regrettable union with Rose have produced a child?

"I...I...I," he stuttered.

"Yes?"

"Why didn't you tell me before now?" he whispered, clenching his fists. He felt oddly cold yet hot all at once, as if he were coming down with a serious virus.

Daisy looked down at her hands. "I wasn't sure you were the father. Rose had lots of boyfriends. I still don't know."

"It doesn't matter. You could have contacted me and told me what you suspected. I would have come back."

"Would you have, Kael? Honestly? What would you have done? Would you have married Rose?"

Kael squirmed in misery. His mind whirled with Daisy's questions. Could Travis really be his son?

"Probably not," Kael replied grimly. "When I, when we... well, you know. I swear to you, Daisy, that night I thought Rose was you."

"I really don't care."

"I know I hurt you deeply—"

Daisy raised both palms. "It doesn't matter. There's no point rehashing the past. What's done is done."

Kael ran his hand over his jaw. "You're right. The question is, where do we go from here?"

"Excuse me?" Daisy raised an eyebrow. Was that fear he saw flit across her face? "What do you mean 'we'?"

"I have to know if Travis is my son."

"Look, it's better to leave well enough alone. I've raised him for over six years by myself. I can do it for the next twelve. There's no point troubling yourself at this late date."

"Yes, you've done an excellent job of raising Travis, but every child deserves to know his father."

"Not a father who'll just abandon him again," Daisy muttered.

"What's that supposed to mean?" Anger coursed through Kael. Daisy had done wrong by not telling him he might be a father. He'd never really thought about having children before, but now everything was different.

"Come on, Kael. You were right to leave Rascal. We both know you're not the *Father Knows Best* type. You've got too much wanderlust in your veins, and you're too irresponsible to be a good dad."

"Dammit, Daisy, you're writing me off without giving me the chance to show you I've changed."

"There's a scorched alfalfa field and a hundred thousand dead bees that say you haven't changed one whit." Her eyes were liquid fire, but Kael was just as angry. He felt used, betrayed, and disrespected by the woman he'd once loved.

"Fine. Think what you will. But know this, I will find out if Travis is my son. First thing

Monday morning, we're going to Rascal for a blood test and don't you dare try to stand in my way!"

🐝  5  🐝

S tunned, Daisy stared at Kael.

Gone was the easy smile, the casual countenance, the teasing light in his hazel eyes. In his stead stood a scowling, rigid-shouldered stranger with a harsh, narrow gaze and a determined set to his jaw.

His light-brown hair was in disarray from where he'd stripped off the bee hat, one errant lock sticking straight up in back. He still wore the zippered coveralls, and a streak of soot smudged one cheek.

He looked like a warrior. Stalwart, unwavering, tense, and ready for combat.

Meeting Kael's challenging glare, Daisy felt the color drain from her face. She wet her lips with the tip of her tongue. "Wh-what are you suggesting?"

"I'm not suggesting anything. I'm putting you on notice. I *will* discover the truth about Travis."

Panic, unlike anything she had ever experienced, scrambled through her in an adrenaline surge.

She raised her chin defiantly. "What if I refuse?"

"Then I'll retain a lawyer. You don't have the resources to fight me on this, Daisy."

Claustrophobia gripped her chest in a tight squeeze. For six and a half years, she'd lived in terror of this moment. Now her greatest fear had come to pass, and the expression on Kael's face told her he would not be thwarted.

If he pursued this issue as fiercely as he rode bulls, she was in serious trouble. She had to do something.

"That's such a selfish attitude," she said, grasping at straws, anything to throw him off balance and make him think twice.

"Excuse me!" Kael raised his voice. "You're calling *me* selfish when you've been hoarding my son from me for years."

"We don't know that he is your son, do we?"

"And whose fault is that?"

"Yours." She matched his hostile tone. "You're the one who ran off without a backward glance for either me or Rose."

"I would never have left if I'd have known about the baby."

"Ha!" Tears burned her eyelids and came dangerously close to slipping down her cheeks. As she had during every adversity in her life, Daisy mentally braced herself for impact. "Easy for you to say now."

"That's why I want a blood test. To make things right."

"See. You *are* selfish."

"Why is that selfish?"

"Because you're only thinking of your wants and desires. Of your redemption, not what's best for Travis."

"Oh-ho, now wait a minute." Kael held up a stop sign palm. "My only concern is my son."

"Then why would you subject him to a blood test?"

"To discover the truth."

Daisy shook her head and crossed her arms over her chest. Did she sound as desperate as she felt? "No. I can't allow it. He's too young."

"Having blood drawn isn't pleasant, but he'll get over the pain. Will he get over not knowing his father?"

"It's not the needle stick that concerns me."

Kael arched an eyebrow. "Yeah?"

"Are you going to explain to him the complexity of his conception? Because I'm certainly not going to tell him the truth about his mother."

Silence more deafening than the loudest noise crashed about her ears. Kael's eyes blazed pure fire. He clenched his fists. The veins on his forehead bulged. She'd never seen him so angry. A bizarre thrill coursed through her.

Kael took a deep breath and swept his gaze south toward the charred alfalfa field. "I'm not backing down on this, Daisy. I've got to know if Travis is my son, and I can't wait until he's eighteen. I've already missed out on six years as it is. Do you have any idea how that makes me feel?"

At this point, she really didn't care how Kael felt. Had he considered her feelings when he'd left town? Had he even thought of her once in the past seven years? She doubted it. He had a one-track mind—bull riding. She'd always been a pale second.

"Why don't you stop and think about Travis for one minute. What do you think will go through that little mind when you tell him that you might be his daddy? He's bound to wonder where you've been all this time and why you abandoned him. Have you given that matter any thought?"

Kael ran a palm down his face. "Daisy, you've hit me with this out of the blue. I haven't had time to absorb any of it. I'm operating on gut instinct. I say let's have the blood test done and don't tell Travis what it's for until we know for sure I'm his father."

"I'm not lying to him."

"I didn't ask you to lie." Kael gave an exasperated sigh. "Just tell him the doctor needs to run some test."

"He's a smart kid. He's going to want to know why."

"Stall him, Daisy. You're good at it. Lord knows you stalled me long enough."

Her face heated at his words. "I suppose that's why you slept with Rose. Your hormones got the better of you."

He glared at her. "I'm not going to dignify that with a reply." He shucked off the coveralls, stepped out of them, and folded them under his arm. "I'll be here at seven o'clock on Monday morning. You better hold Travis out of school and have him ready to go or I promise you, there'll be hell to pay."

❧

A ROTTEN SENSATION LAY IN KAEL'S BELLY LIKE A LEAD CASKET. ALL Saturday and Sunday he'd vacillated between anger, resentment, sadness, and melancholy.

He would think about how Daisy had deceived him, and he'd grind his teeth, then he would remind himself she'd only been trying to protect herself and her son. Much as he hated to admit it, he probably wouldn't have been a good father at twenty-one.

But dammit, she'd deprived him of the opportunity to try. And now? What kind of father would he be? He already felt a rush of unexpected love for the red-haired boy who looked so much like Daisy.

*Hold up, Carmody*, he reminded himself once more. Don't get too soft on the boy until you know for sure.

But that sensible note of caution couldn't stop his heart from doing flip-flops when he sneaked over the property line dividing the Carmody ranch from Hightower Honey Farm and watched the boy play in his backyard.

"My son." Kael tried the words out loud. They felt alien...but nice.

Hunkering in the grass, watching Travis while he hung upside down from the branch of an old oak tree, Kael felt overwhelming guilt.

Guilt tightened like a corkscrew. Kael winced. He'd never meant to hurt anyone. Not Rose. Not Daisy and certainly not this innocent little boy. But if Travis was indeed his son, his ugly sins were there to claim.

Dang. He'd made so many mistakes. How could he atone for them all?

Travis whistled tunelessly. The poor kid seemed lonely. He was quiet. Solemn and solitary.

He should be playing baseball, hide-and-go-seek, or tag. Kael ached to reach out to him, to show him the things boys learned from their fathers.

The child needed a male role model. Daisy was doing her best, but nothing could replace a man's influence, and it was obvious she had more on her plate than she could chew.

Whereas Kael had all the time in the world.

Was he making the right decision, demanding a blood test? What if he was Travis' father? What would the boy think of him then? How could he explain his absence without casting either Rose or Daisy in a bad light?

Kael blew out his breath. What a mess! A lonely boy without a father. A hardworking woman trying to make ends meet. A wealthy cowboy, aimless and unhappy, without any goals left in life. Sad, really, that they were isolated from each other when they should be together.

The thought caught in Kael's mind and hammered at him. They could be a family. Yeah. Sure. As if Daisy would ever forgive him.

His fault. All his fault.

No. Although he certainly wasn't blameless, Daisy had brought a lot of this upon herself. If she'd been honest with him, he could have been here to help her through the hard times.

Daisy had known nothing but hard work her entire life. The woman had no idea how to have fun.

It was a wonder, Kael marveled, that he and Daisy had ever gotten together at all. They were such opposites. She was stable, solid, dependable. He was flexible, rootless, wayward. She, quiet. He, wild. Daisy was self-contained, while he'd hungered for the limelight.

Of course, she'd been the one person who hadn't fallen at his feet, and he'd respected her for that. In fact, Kael remembered with a wry smile, he'd had a devil of a time convincing her to even go out with him.

He'd lived next door to Daisy Hightower all his life, but he'd never thought of her as a woman until the summer she turned sixteen just a few short months before her parents' fatal automobile accident.

He'd been checking on the cattle for his father when he spotted Daisy working in the apiary. Her long red hair, unencumbered by a bee veil, glistening in the early morning sunlight. She'd looked like a fairy princess — lithe, lissome, and completely captivating.

Her lean, graceful body encased in white coveralls that could not camouflage her spectacular figure. The sight of her had taken his breath. His body's response had been swift and immediate.

He'd known it was Daisy right off the bat. Rose had little interest in the bees. She spent her spare time riding horses and chasing boys. No, from the very start it had always been Daisy.

She'd been humming under her breath, a soft, lilting melody, and Kael recalled thinking she was the most incredible creature he'd ever seen.

Forever cocky and sure of himself, he'd sauntered over to the fence row and called out to her.

"Hey, good-looking."

She'd sent him a look that would have withered grapes into raisins and kept going about her business.

"Perhaps I should have said, Miss Stuck-Up," he goaded.

Daisy ignored him.

He'd flung a leg across the fence and climbed over onto the Hightower property.

"You're trespassing, Mr. Carmody," she had said without even looking up from her work. Bees buzzed around her like she was their queen. Kael didn't blame them for their devotion. She was the most majestic girl he'd ever seen. Aloof, detached, poised, and serene.

"What are you going to do about it, Miss Hightower?" he'd asked, coming toward her.

She'd raised her head, and her eyes met his.

Even now, years later, the recollection of that exchange raised something deep within him—an odd sensation of panic and euphoria as if he'd met his match and she was far too good for him.

"You really aren't interested in tangling with my bees, are you, Mr. Carmody?"

"You're kidding, right?" He'd allowed a killer grin to spread across his face.

She never cracked a smile. "Am I?"

"You wouldn't have your attack bees sting the greatest bull rider ever born, now would you?"

"I might. If such a man was in the vicinity."

"I'm the greatest bull rider ever born." He'd thrust out his chest in a preening gesture, an arrogant eighteen-year-old.

She'd been completely unimpressed. Daisy had rolled her eyes and turned her back to him. "Ever heard of humility?"

Quickly, he'd circled around to face her again.

"Hey, can you really make the bees sting someone?"

"Try me."

He hadn't braved to take the dare, but from that moment on, he hadn't been able to stop thinking about Daisy.

He'd pestered her, asking her out two or three times a week.

She'd fed him a passel of excuses. Most of them legitimate: she was too busy helping out on the honey farm in her spare time; she was an honor student and had to maintain a high grade-point average in order to get into the college of her choice; her parents were old-fashioned and wouldn't allow her to date until she was seventeen.

But Kael kept after her until she told him the truth—that she just wasn't interested in someone stupid enough to risk his neck by climbing onto the back of a bull.

Rebuffed for the first time, Kael refused to take rejection lying down.

Daisy had been cool, distant, but once a while, she'd offered him just enough encouragement. A smile, a chuckle, a coy side-ways glance. Whenever she'd come to the rodeo arena to watch Rose race barrels, Kael flirted with her. Daisy would pick up a book and pretend to read.

"Are you shy?" Kael asked one day. "Or just rude."

"Rude," she'd answered.

"All the other girls think I'm one heck of a guy, why don't you?"

"Do the words *arrogant jerk* mean anything to you?"

"Ah, come on, Daisy, give me a chance. I'm not so bad."

"Says you."

"One date with me, and you'll change your opinion," he wheedled. "How about it?"

"Don't hold your breath, Kael."

He gave her his best "sad puppy dog" expression. "Please."

"Why don't you quit bothering me and go out with Rose. For some crazy reason, she thinks you're charming."

"I don't want to go out with Rose. I want to go out with you."

She'd given him a dubious look. "Everyone wants to go out with Rose."

"Not me."

"Why not? We look exactly alike. Pretend she's me."

"I don't want to date you for your beauty."

Both Daisy's eyebrows had shot up on her forehead. "Oh, that's believable."

"I can't help it. You intrigue me."

"Only because I won't go out with you."

Kael shrugged. "Gotta confess, I love a challenge."

"All right." Daisy sighed. "If I agree to have a cold drink with you, will you promise to leave me alone after that?"

He'd been so happy, he'd tossed his hat in the air and shouted, "Yippee."

His happiness, however, had been short-lived. Before he and Daisy had had a chance to sip that cold drink together in the worn vinyl booth at an old-fashioned soda fountain inside the Rascal drugstore, Daisy's parents had been killed in an automobile accident.

For the first few weeks, he'd stayed out of her way, giving the sogginess of immediate grief time to ease. Then he'd shown up on her doorstep, offering to help around the honey farm.

Daisy, as he had expected she would, refused. But Rose and Aunt Peavy had embraced his help, giving him chores to do and rewarding him with home-cooked meals. Eventually, Daisy had come to rely on him, too, even though she never admitted it.

Kael shook away the memory and smiled wistfully from where he crouched beside the fence row. He gazed across the pasture, studying the child that might be his son as the boy climbed higher into the branches of the ancient oak tree.

A few minutes later, Daisy came out on the patio and called Travis in for supper. Kael's stomach scaled his throat at the sight of her.

Lordy, but she was beautiful—her red hair caught in her

signature ponytail and her lean body wrapped in tight blue jeans and a faded western shirt. She wore no makeup or jewelry, but Daisy didn't need such things. Her loveliness was the natural kind that outshone any professional runway model or sleek, sophisticated actress.

Daisy was a down-to-earth woman. She didn't mind getting her hands dirty or breaking a fingernail or sweating. She worked. Hard. Had her whole life. Strange, really, how she and her identical twin sister, Rose, had come from the same background but turned out so differently.

He swallowed hard.

Daisy placed her hands on her hips and looked briefly toward the ranch before turning her attention to the apiary. He caught a glimpse of her face. Her eyes were worried, her mouth pressed into a firm line.

How he longed to put a smile on those lovely lips, but it seemed as if he just kept adding to her suffering.

What he wouldn't give to hear her laugh again! The woman roused in him such an intense fighting spirit. A spirit Kael had only previously experienced on the back of a bucking bull.

Actually, Miss Daisy was much more dangerous than any rip-snorting Brahma. The bull might have macerated his leg, but Daisy had mangled his heart.

Kael still felt the pain. A deep lingering ache he feared might never heal. Such a crying shame. They had once had so much potential. Could they ever hope to bridge the chasm separating them?

Daisy sank her hands on her hips and called to Travis again.

Observing her, Kael tried his best to ignore the burning in his gut. Seven years, and his unintentional betrayal stretched between them. He lost his window of opportunity with her. The most he could hope for was to become a good father to his child.

Daisy and Travis disappeared into the house.

LORI WILDE

Kael sighed and got to his feet. The odor of charred grass clung to the air. He dusted his hands on the seat of his pants.

Perhaps Daisy was right. Maybe he should simply leave well enough alone and not proceed with the blood test. Yet part of him balked at the idea. He'd made a lot of mistakes, and he didn't want to compound them. Whether Daisy liked it or not, he had to know if Travis was his son.

۞

DAISY PUT OFF TELLING TRAVIS ABOUT THE BLOOD TEST FOR AS LONG as she dared. Sunday evening, after supper was over and the dishes had been washed, she called him into the kitchen.

Aunt Peavy was snoring gently on the couch, the television set tuned in to a rerun of *The Golden Girls*. A stack of unpaid bills sat on the sideboard awaiting Daisy's attention, and the clock on the wall ticked loudly as if counting down her fate.

"Sit down, son." Daisy indicated the chair with a nod.

"Did I do something wrong?" Travis fretted.

Unfortunately, the child took after her. She wished he wasn't such a worry wart.

"No, honey, I just need to talk to you."

"Is it about money?"

Daisy heaved a deep breath. "Sweetheart, you don't have to be concerned about money. I'll take care of that."

Travis said nothing, just eased into the chair and stared down at his hands.

Clearing her throat, Daisy wondered how to begin. "I'm keeping you out of school tomorrow," she said at last.

The boy's head came up. "How come?"

"I'm taking you to the doctor in Rascal."

Travis' face blanched pale. "What's the matter?"

"You need to have some blood work done."

"I'm not sick."

Panic shone in her son's eyes, and Daisy knew she'd taken the wrong track. Travis was too smart to be easily assuaged, but he was too young to be told the whole truth.

"No, you're not sick." She quickly backpedaled. "This is a different kind of test."

Travis frowned. "Do I have to?"

Daisy swallowed. *Dang you, Kael.* Her only goal in life was to take care of Travis. "I think it would be a good idea."

"But why?"

"Well," Daisy hedged, postulating the excuse she'd devised over the past few days. "Your teacher has been a little worried about you." This was true enough. On more than one occasion Travis' teacher had expressed concern over the boy's quiet disposition.

His brows drew down in a frown. "Worried about me? How come?"

"You've been so sad lately, and you hardly ever play with the other kids. I thought it might be a good idea to see the doctor to make sure something isn't wrong."

Travis studied his feet. "Wanna know why I'm sad?"

Her heart caught in her chest as his words rent a hole through her. "Yes, sweetie. I want to know everything about how you're feeling."

"I'm sad 'cause I don't have a daddy like everyone else. Even kids whose parents are divorced got daddies, but not me. Jimmy's even got two daddies!"

"Oh, baby, come here." Daisy gathered him to her breast.

His despair cleaved her right in two. How long had this been bothering Travis? Poor kid. Perhaps it wouldn't be such a bad thing if Kael turned out to be his father.

"Maybe you'll have a daddy someday."

Travis face brightened. "You think so?"

"Who knows, maybe I'll get married someday."

"Really?"

Daisy smiled. "Stranger things have happened. In the meantime, I still think we need to have you checked out by a doctor. Okay?"

"Okay." Travis nodded.

"Come on," she said, "time for bed."

She ushered him through the kitchen, her mind whirling. The boy deserved to know his father. But Daisy dreaded what Kael might do if he was Travis' father.

He was a wealthy man accustomed to getting his way. Would he try to take control of the boy's upbringing? Or worse, would he attempt to wrest custody from her entirely? Daisy clenched her fists. Anxiety, dark and cloying, took hold of her and refused to let go.

Travis slipped his small hand in hers, and Daisy clutched it tightly. They ascended the stairs together. Mother and son. Alone. As they had been for over six years.

And until recently they'd gotten along just fine. Or perhaps she had just wanted to think they were doing fine. She'd had no idea Travis was pining for a father. Daisy bit her lip. Had she been wrong all this time, keeping Travis from Kael?

*What about Kael?* a voice in the back of her head asked. *How does he fit into this picture?*

Indeed, what about him? Their relationship had ended a long time ago. The man couldn't still harbor feelings for her. He'd never once tried to contact her after he left.

*Why not? You still harbor feelings for him.*

*I do not!* Daisy denied hotly.

And even if she did have the faintest of feelings for the man, she couldn't forgive him.

So why, when Kael kissed her on Friday afternoon in the bee field, had Daisy been transported back in time? What was it about his lips that drove all common sense from her mind? Why did the man possess the ability to turn her mind to instant oatmeal with a mere glance?

For that brief moment when he kissed her, she'd been nineteen again and falling deeply in love.

Her reaction to Kael's kiss had reminded her what a fool she'd been to lose her head over a footloose male with a roving eye. It was only her prideful nature that had prevented her from declaring her love to keep him from leaving town seven years ago. Now she was so glad she hadn't.

This way Kael would never know for sure how she felt about him. And that's exactly where she wanted him, squarely off balance.

Because if Travis was his son, then the man had her over a barrel. She'd have to let him see the boy. Much as she hated to admit it, he needed a paternal influence. And once Kael was back in her life, would she be stupid enough to fall in love with him again?

Dang.

She was torn, conflicted. She wanted Travis to know his father and yet she really didn't want to share her child with anyone. Especially someone as pushy and opinionated as Kael.

Running Travis' bath water while he shucked off his T-shirt and blue jeans, Daisy tested the temperature with her elbow before dumping in the bubble bath. The fresh smell of soap teased her nose, and bubbles floated gaily above the tub.

At this point, there was only one thing left to do. Pray furiously that Kael was not the father of her boy.

# 6

For once Kael's infamous cool failed him.

He could straddle a wild bull without a second thought, but the idea of becoming a ready-made father had him shaking in his boots.

In the matter of a few hours, the course of his life might be irrevocably changed forever, altered in ways he couldn't imagine.

Early morning sun cast a soft orange glow over the high desert when Kael pulled into Daisy's driveway. His stomach was wadded in such knots he'd been unable to eat breakfast, and he felt oddly tongue-tied. How much had Daisy told the boy about the trip into Rascal?

Daisy and Travis waited for him on the front porch. With their solemn faces, they looked as if they were headed for a funeral.

Travis wore starched blue jeans and a crisp white shirt, and Daisy had on a knee-length, black dress that showed off her shapely legs. Her vibrant hair was upswept in a severe bun, and her feet were shod in sensible flats.

Kael caught his breath at the sight. Even in such plain garb, she was a stunner. He opened the door and climbed out at the same time they walked over to meet him.

"Morning." Kael doffed his Stetson.

"Good morning," Daisy replied primly.

Travis mumbled something.

They all three pretended to study their feet.

"Thanks for taking us to the doctor's office," Daisy mumbled. "We really appreciate you giving us a ride, Mr. Carmody, since the green monster is out of commission."

Kael angled her a look. *Mr. Carmody?* Was this a cue to how she wanted him to behave around Travis? What *had* she told the boy about this doctor visit?

"No problem."

Travis squinted against the sun edging up the horizon and peered at Kael. "I gotta have a blood test."

"I heard." Kael nodded. He searched Daisy's face for clues, but she carefully avoided his gaze.

"It's making sure I'm not sick or anything."

"That sounds like a good idea." Nervously, Kael clasped his hands together, the magnitude of the situation registering for the first time. He was about to discover if he had a six-year-old son.

"You ready to hit the road?" he asked.

Without waiting for an answer, he opened the passenger door and ushered them inside. Lordy, the fifteen-mile jaunt to Rascal was beginning to look like a fifteen-thousand-mile trek. He got in and started the pickup, racking his brain for small talk.

Daisy stared straight ahead. She sat pressed against the passenger door as if ready to use it as an escape hatch, her body language declaring very loudly "touch me not."

What else did he expect? Kael figured she'd only agreed to this blood test out of a sense of fairness to Travis and because he'd threatened her with a lawsuit. Kael winced. This couldn't be any easier for her than it was for him.

Guilt crawled through him at a slow, tortuous pace. Daisy's whole world had come crashing in around her ears, and it was all his fault. He'd burned her bees, and now he was making her face something she wanted to deny.

Travis sat in the back, and before they'd driven far, he'd fallen fast asleep.

"Kid's tuckered out," Kael commented.

"I'm glad he's asleep. This is going to be rough enough on him."

"It's got to be done, Daisy."

"Why?"

"We both have a right to know the truth," he said.

"What good is knowing the truth?" Daisy asked. "If you're not going to stick around?"

Kael paused to check his temper before responding. "I've changed, Daisy."

She turned her head and snorted indelicately. "Oh, yeah? Since when?"

Kael stroked his jaw and stared out across the pickup's hood. "I suppose since my accident. There's nothing like having your kneecap shattered to give you a whole new perspective."

"And riding a motorcycle through an alfalfa field was the action of a mature man?"

"The fire wasn't intentional."

"Like you didn't intentionally take Rose into the barn that night?"

"Daisy," he growled. "Leave well enough alone."

"What do you expect from me, Kael? I don't hear one word from you in seven years, now suddenly you want me to make room for daddy?"

Anger that matched his own sparked in her eyes. How many times had she stood her ground and challenged him like that? And how many times had her spicy nature roused him? Kael's groin tightened in response. Dammit, she didn't even realize the power she wielded over him.

"You told me you never wanted to see me again. Remember?" He spoke softly as the pain of their parting flooded through him.

Yes, seven years ago he'd been selfish and immature. His mind had been set on riding bulls and proving to himself he was worthy of his father's name. Plus, he'd wanted to satisfy his wanderlust before settling down and having a family. But he'd always known Daisy was the woman he wanted to marry—the girl he hoped would eventually become his wife and bear his children. He'd never wanted Rose, not even when he had her.

"What was I supposed to do?" he asked softly.

Daisy shrugged. Her jaw trembled. Was she about to cry? Tough-as-nails Daisy?

"Are you okay?" He reached for her, but she flinched, and he withdrew his hand. "I know this has got to be hard for you."

"Don't patronize me." She folded her arms over her chest.

Kael sighed. He couldn't win. "I promise I'm not going to take Travis away from you, if that's what you're worried about. I just want to know my son."

"Let's save this discussion until we know for sure."

He nodded. She was right. He slowed as they entered Rascal city limits. Up ahead, he saw the sign for Balmorhea Springs.

"Remember that time we went skinny-dipping?" Kael grinned.

"No."

"Sure, you do. It was after—"

"I prefer not to think about the past," she interrupted. "It's full of painful memories, and there's nothing I can do to change that."

"Daisy, I'm sorry for all the ways I've wronged you."

"Apologies are easy for you, Kael. It's the consequences you have a hard time dealing with." She glanced over her shoulder at the back seat.

Kael studied the child in the rearview mirror. Travis' hair was

69

darker than his mother's, rusty instead of flame-colored. A dusting of freckles dotted his cheeks and nose, just like Daisy's. And like hers, the sweep of his eyelashes was long and pale.

Travis breathed quietly, his slender chest rising and falling as he slept. He seemed so small, so fragile. The sight tugged at Kael.

"I can't believe you kept your suspicions about Travis from me for so long." He was trying not to sound bitter, but he wasn't sure he succeeded.

"Shh," she cautioned, laying an index finger against her lips as Travis stirred.

Kael clamped his mouth shut. He hadn't wanted to admit it, not even to himself, but from the moment he'd returned to Rascal, memories had nipped at his heels. When he'd seen Daisy again and discovered her son might be his child, he had been fighting some pretty crazy fantasies. Visions of them as a family. He and Daisy and Travis. Living together, running the honey farm, loving each other the way it should be.

*What about your rodeo career? Where does that fit into your cozy family life?*

Heck, he was twenty-eight, plenty old enough to grow up and surrender his dreams. He'd risen to the top tier of the PBR. He'd ridden the best bulls in the world. What else was there left to accomplish in the arena?

Two questions remained unanswered. The answer to the first question would lead him down one path, the solution to the other pointed in the opposite direction.

One: Would his knee heal?

Two: Was Travis really his son?

TWO DAYS PASSED. TIME CRAWLED AS DAISY WAITED TO HEAR THE results of the blood test. She spent as much time with the bees as she could, reorganizing the depleted hives and planning her next move.

Despite Kael's assurance that he wouldn't try to take Travis from her, Daisy wasn't so sure she believed him. Kael and his family were rich. He could hire the best lawyers. If he took a notion to fight her...

Her heart wrenched. Would he really do that to her?

"Daisy!"

She raised her head and saw Aunt Peavy waving at her from the backyard. Shucking her bee veil, Daisy walked away from the apiary.

Sweeping her hand through her hair, she licked her dry lips. The bees buzzed erratically around their condensed colonies, still shocked from the fire.

"Telephone," Aunt Peavy said. "It's the laboratory."

This was it. The moment she'd been dreading since Travis' birth. Somewhere deep inside her, she'd always known the truth. That Kael and Rose had indeed produced a child.

*Her* child.

Aunt Peavy reached out and squeezed her arm. "Whatever happens, Daisy, it's going to be okay."

"I wish I could be so sure."

"You're the strongest person I know. You'll come through this with flying colors."

Daisy nodded and squared her shoulders. What choice did she have? Wiping the dirt from her shoes on the welcome mat, she went into the house and with trembling fingers, picked up the phone.

"Hello?" Her voice came out dry and scratchy, her hand curling tightly around the receiver. Sudden dizziness made her head swim, and her vision blurred.

"Is this Ms. Daisy Hightower?"

"Yes, it is." Daisy blinked, cleared her throat, and placed a palm flat against the table to brace herself.

"This is Gina from Kelon Laboratories in San Antonio."

"Uh-huh."

"We have the results of the paternity testing on your son Travis."

"Go ahead." It took every ounce of strength Daisy possessed to say it.

"The test came back ninety-nine percent conclusive that Kael Carmody is the father of your son."

⚜

THERE WAS ONLY ONE THING TO DO. KAEL POCKETED HIS CELL PHONE and grabbed his Stetson. He was going to ask Daisy to marry him and convince her it was the right thing to do.

He was Travis' father, and the child needed a man in his life. Daisy was in deep financial straits, and he had the money to provide for her and his son.

And bottom line, he still loved Daisy. It didn't matter if she didn't love him anymore or that she could not forgive him for sleeping with Rose. She had two very good reasons for marrying him, and Kael was not about to give up until he won.

The feelings swimming through Kael were foreign.

A surge of fatherly pride followed by the conviction that he was inept and ill-equipped for the job. He didn't know anything about being a parent. For the first time, someone would depend on him, and that scared Kael more than ten dozen bucking bulls.

It was a humbling and awe-inspiring thought.

He was a father.

A dad.

And he'd missed out on so much.

Fear over his own performance as a parent dissipated as a hard chunk of anger wedged inside his head. His son was already over six years old!

He'd been cheated. Robbed of the most precious moments

of infancy and early childhood. He would never get up in the middle of the night and rock his newborn son. He would never see Travis' first steps or hear his first words.

Regret, heavy as a knife blade, split him straight through the heart.

The more he thought about it, the madder he got. Daisy and Rose had been wrong not to contact him all those years ago and tell him he might be a father.

So very wrong.

Stalking out of the house, Kael grit his teeth. He jumped into the pickup and gunned the engine. His hands shook, and his foot fumbled with the clutch. The pickup shot forward, then died.

The catalog of missed "firsts" continued to tumble through Kael's mind. He started the engine again and rammed the accelerator to the floorboard. The truck leaped onto the road, grinding gears and spewing gravel.

First smile, first baby tooth, first birthday cake. First Christmas, first skinned knee, first day of school.

Kael slammed his fist on the steering wheel and accidentally honked the horn. A farmer, riding a slow-moving tractor on the roadside, drove into the ditch to avoid him.

He slowed and gave the guy a sheepish wave. His neighbor, Keegan Winslow. *Sorry, Keegan.*

As long as he'd had the element of doubt about Travis' parentage, Kael had been able to remain calm, but once that tech from the lab had removed all but a one percent margin of error, his paternal instincts kicked in.

The tires squealed as he braked to a stop in Daisy's driveway and leaped from the vehicle. He dashed up the porch, ignoring the ache in his leg, and pounded on her front door.

Aunt Peavy appeared, a frown knitting her brow.

"Where's Daisy?" he demanded.

"Here now, Kael," the elderly lady scolded, shaking a finger in his face. "You settle down right this minute. Daisy is just as disturbed as you are."

"Where is she?" Kael repeated. He was long past the point of being cajoled.

Aunt Peavy must have read his intention on his face because she opened the door and stepped aside. "She's upstairs in her room. But I swear if you upset her, I'm going to come up there and whack you with my broom."

"Me? Upset her? How do you think it feels, Aunt Peavy, to discover out of nowhere that you have a six-year-old son?"

Aunt Peavy sniffed and glared at him over the top of her thick glasses. "If you'd have come home once in the past seven years, maybe she would have told you."

Kael stuffed his hands in his pockets. "She should have told me, anyway."

"After the way you hurt her? I'm surprised she'll even speak to you at all."

He drew in a deep breath. How had his life gotten so complicated? Things used to be so simple. Riding a bull. Staying on for eight seconds. No sweat.

Except, even before his accident, Kael had grown bored with the whole process. He'd already conquered the top of the bull riding world. What else was left? Making a comeback from a crippling injury? Besides, if he gave up rodeoing, what would he do with himself?

Be a father?

Kael cringed. He was facing some hard choices.

"If you'll excuse me, Aunt Peavy, Daisy and I have a lot of things to discuss."

"Just you mind your tongue with her," Aunt Peavy reminded him. "I'm an old lady, and she and Travis are all I have left."

Nodding, Kael edged past her and headed for the stairs.

Daisy and Rose had once shared the first bedroom on the left. Kael laid his hand on the doorknob.

Suddenly, it was very hard to breathe. He was about to cross the threshold into a whole new world of responsibility. With the proposition he was about to offer Daisy, Kael's life as he knew it would cease to exist.

He knocked.

"Come in."

Kael turned the knob and pushed open the door.

The room had changed since the last time Kael had visited it. In those days, there had been twin beds and a stereo system stocked with the latest music. A television set and matching beanbag chairs, brightly colored knickknacks and makeup strewn across the old dressing table.

Today, the room reflected Daisy's solo personality. The flamboyant posters of movie stars and rock legends were gone. The electronic equipment had disappeared as well as the old furnishings.

Everything was simple, direct, and functional. There were no frills, no ruffles, no extravagance. The walls were painted white and adorned only by pictures of Travis, Rose, Aunt Peavy, and Daisy's parents. The small bookcase housed numerous tomes on beekeeping and farm repair, but there were no novels or biographies, no entertaining reading of any kind.

But it was Daisy that seized his attention.

She sat cross-legged in the middle of her queen-size bed, her face buried in her hands. Her hair was pulled in a ponytail, and she wore a red T-shirt and a pair of cutoff blue jeans that showed off her long, slender legs. A box of tissues rested beside her.

"Daisy?" The anger that had carried him this far quietly evaporated as he realized she'd been crying. He'd never seen her cry, not even when her parents had been killed. Taken aback, he simply stood there.

She sniffled and raised her head. Her eyes were moist, her nose reddened, but her shoulders were set firm and brave.

"Kael."

"The lab called me." He hesitated in the doorway, his hand still worrying the knob.

"I know. Me too."

Their eyes fastened on each other.

"I'm a dad."

Daisy's heart stuttered against her breastbone. The moment of truth had arrived. Her worst suspicions had been confirmed. The man she had loved for so long was indeed the father of her twin sister's child. That awful night over seven years ago had come back to haunt them both with a vengeance.

"May I come in?" he asked, his question surprising her.

She'd heard him downstairs talking to Aunt Peavy, his voice raised in anger. She knew Kael was not a man to be thwarted, and she had expected him to come charging into her room like a Brahma on a rampage, demanding joint custody of her son. Instead, he looked rather like a lost little boy himself.

Before she could steel herself, a wash of emotions swamped Daisy. Swallowing hard, she willed herself free of feelings. Denying her heartache was the only way she'd survived all these years. Now was not the time to let down her guard and give in to the quicksand of fear and sadness.

"Come on in," she invited, and he shut the door behind him.

The small room shrunk in his presence. Daisy nervously fingered a shredded tissue.

"We've got to talk."

She waved a hand at the rocking chair, resigned to the inevitable.

Kael ignored the chair and stepped closer to the bed. He limped slightly, and the evidence of his wound yanked at something deep inside Daisy.

For the longest time, she'd even refused to date him because he was a bull rider. She'd seen no percentage in becoming involved with a man who courted danger. Why get mixed up with extra trouble when life already offered so much grief?

And she'd been right about him, too. But that knowledge did nothing to ease her suffering.

Even though common sense had warned her off, she'd been attracted to him. Just like now. There was something irresistible about Kael. From that wide, cocky grin to his nonchalant stride, he made a girl yearn to be kissed.

The way he was looking at her didn't help matters, either. He pushed aside her pillows and lowered himself down on the bed beside her.

The aroma of this male—zest and sunshine, soap and leather —descended upon her. Rousing not only long-dormant memories but her sexual desire as well.

Daisy hiccuped back salty tears and struggled to calm her rapidly fluttering pulse. No man

had ever awakened her the way Kael did, and the control he wielded bothered her. For over seven years, she'd fought that power and stupidly believed she'd gotten over him. She was wrong.

"I'm sorry," he said simply. "For all the pain I caused you and Rose and Travis."

She touched the tip of her tongue to her upper lip and sat in stunned silence. She had anticipated his anger. Instead, he was asking for her forgiveness.

"I don't know where to begin," Kael said, "making up for the damage I've caused."

"We've got to do what's best for Travis," Daisy said.

"I agree." He reached across the bed and took her hand.

His touch, like the Earth's atmosphere to a meteor, sent her splintering into a thousand hot, brittle pieces.

Daisy sucked in her breath through gritted teeth and jerked back.

But it was too late. She'd been stamped by his mark, labeled with the unmistakable imprint of Kael's woman.

"That's why you're going to marry me," he continued.

"Excuse me?" Daisy arched her back and turned to stare him full in the face. "What?" Had she heard him correctly? Was he actually *telling* her she was going to marry him?

## 7

**U**nflinchingly, he met her stare. His hazel eyes, so much like Travis', reflected back at her, clear and unwavering.

Yes, this was the cocky son of a gun she remembered. From the very first time he'd asked her out, Kael tried to bend her to his will.

Well, she was having none of it. Daisy Anne had plenty of grit on her own! She didn't need a man, especially someone as high-handed as Kael telling her what to do.

She'd survived her parents' tragic deaths and kept the honey farm on track. She'd overcome Rose's betrayal and Travis' unexpected arrival. She'd kept on trucking down life's perilous highway despite her twin's drug overdose and Aunt Peavy's cancer scare last year.

"It's the best thing," he said, his words earnest.

"According to you."

"We need each other."

"Like heck we do."

"Let me do right by you, Daisy." His eyes were sincere,

pleading. "Let me be a father to my son. Let me help you rebuild the honey farm. Let's make a real family together. You, me, and Travis."

"Why should I provide your redemption? You weren't there when I needed you."

Kael thumped his fist against the headboard. "I'm here now. Doesn't that count for anything?"

"No. You're only here because you've lost everything else." She stared at his bum leg.

Kael blew out his breath and rubbed both palms along the top of his thighs. "I know the situation is not ideal, but we could make the best of it. I want to make the best of it. Please, Daisy, give it some thought."

"Do you expect me to believe you've changed that much?"

"I have."

Daisy pushed herself off the bed and onto her feet. Settling her hands on her hips, she narrowed her eyes. "Who are you trying to kid? Me or yourself?"

"I had every intention of coming back home for you after my rodeo career was over," he said.

"Was that before or after you took my sister to bed?"

"Darn it, Daisy." Kael got to his feet and lowered his face to hers. The pain and hurt in his eyes matched her own. "I swear I thought Rose was you."

"That's convenient, now that Rose isn't here to defend herself."

"Your sister seduced me on purpose. Don't you get it? How else did Rose know I was at Kelly's Bar?"

"Where else would you be celebrating another victory?" For seven years, Daisy had needed to blame Kael. To hold him accountable instead of facing the painful truth. That her own twin sister had purposely set out to make love to Daisy's boyfriend just to hurt her. Because she *had* talked to Rose that night.

She had told her twin about the big blowup between her and Kael. It would have been so easy for Rose to pretend to be her. They were identical twins after all, and as children, they'd swapped places often. Especially late at night, with Kael flying high on his win and celebratory drinks.

"Rose was dressed in your clothes and wearing her hair in a ponytail. She knew exactly what she was doing, Daisy."

"That's right, go ahead, pin it all on a dead woman." She held on to her anger because she wanted so badly to forgive him. To make a fresh start. But was that smart? She was so afraid to trust him. He had the power to pulverize her heart to powder.

"You know Rose had been after me for years. Long before you and I ever started going out together."

Daisy had no comeback. She'd suspected her twin sister had intentionally seduced Kael while he was vulnerable.

But even if her sister had seduced him, that in no way exonerated Kael. What would have happened if he *had* made love to her instead of Rose, and she had been the one to get pregnant? Would he have come back and married her? She would never know, would she?

"Daisy, you were the one issuing ultimatums, demanding marriage or nothing. Well, here's your chance; I want to marry you now."

"You don't want to marry *me*. You're just feeling guilty. You think you can come in and take over, become this great dad. It doesn't work that way, buddy. Parenting is difficult work, and it's going to take time to build Travis' trust."

"I'm aware of that," Kael murmured. "But give me a chance to prove myself. Can you do that?"

The nineteen-year-old girl in her wanted to cry, *yes, yes*. But she'd been through too much to hang her hopes on fate or the fantasy of true love. Did that make her hard?

He leaned in so close their noses almost touched.

Being this near him sent warm tingles throughout her whole body. How could she be so turned on when she was so upset? One look in those shadowy hazel eyes and her whole body quivered.

Kael must have felt it, too, because in the next instant, he pulled her headlong into his embrace.

Shocked, Daisy froze as his strong arms bunched around her waist and his lips dipped down to seize hers in a kiss so bold, so forceful, her toes curled.

He'd never kissed her like this before.

In the past, his kisses had been teasing, cajoling, frisky, and sassy. They'd been the kisses of a playful kid.

But this? Wow! He was all grown up and one hundred percent male.

The kiss scared the pants off Daisy, and she had a feeling that's precisely what Kael intended.

Trembling, she tried to push away, but her hands knotted ineffectively against his chest as his tongue explored.

He was angry with her. She could taste it on him. Well, dammit, she was angry, too!

Oddly enough, their mingled anger excited as much as it frightened. Daisy tossed her head and growled low in her throat, intending it to be a warning. Instead, muffled by his moist active lips, the noise sounded like a soft moan of desire.

He devoured her. His fingers slid through her hair, and his heart thudded against her chest, while his tongue strummed over her teeth.

Daisy, overwhelmed by the sensations, closed her eyes and let it happen.

She savored the pressure of his arm on her shoulder, delighted in his unique taste, and reveled in his manly scent—all sand, sunshine, and man. When at last she felt courageous enough, she pried opened her eyes to find him staring intently at her.

Simultaneously, her pupils widened, her pulse quickened, and her stomach contracted.

"Stop it," she cried, breaking away from him. "What do you think you're doing?"

"Giving you a taste of what our marriage will be like." His hair was disheveled, his collar askew. His breath was ragged, his eyes murky with passion.

"I'm not going to marry you."

"Not even for the sake of our son?"

That stopped her cold. Daisy frowned and rubbed her forehead. "Even if I did agree to marry you, it would be in name only. A formal marriage of convenience, so we could both get what we wanted."

"Why?"

"Why what?"

"Why does it have to be a marriage in name only?"

"Because I don't want you."

"Is that true?" He studied her face. "Or is it because you're terrified if you give in to your impulses that you'll turn wild like Rose?"

"No!" Daisy denied, but his words hit far too close to home. She had avoided sex because of her sister's wildness.

"I'm asking you to think about it, Daisy. A real marriage. A forever marriage. I know you loved me once..." He paused, locking his gaze on hers. "As much as I loved you. If you give me a chance and agree to be my wife, I promise I'll spend a lifetime showing you and Travis just how much you both mean to me."

"And if I don't?"

He looked so sad it took the breath from her lungs. "Then we'll both spend the rest of our lives with regrets for what might have been."

SHE COULDN'T MARRY KAEL. NOT BECAUSE SHE DIDN'T STILL LOVE him, but precisely because she did. He could damage her in a hundred different ways.

Sucking in a ragged breath, Daisy stared at the tenacious man towering above her. He was cocksure, arrogant, and smug beyond belief. And she didn't trust him. Not for one minute.

Not that she doubted that he believed what he was saying… for now. He'd always been a passionate guy. But she just didn't know if he had what it took for the long haul. Marriage was not easy. Neither was parenthood.

"I mean what I said," he warned, placing a hand on the door-frame, barring her exit. "I want to marry you. So start getting used to the idea."

Daisy stood stock-still, fists knotted at her sides, mind whirling as she weighed her options. If she refused to let him see Travis, he'd have her in court before she knew what hit her. Although she doubted a judge would take Travis from her, Kael would probably get joint custody.

"Daisy, will you marry me?"

"No." She raised her chin and forced herself to meet his stare.

"Not even for Travis?"

She swallowed. Was she being a bad mother by turning down his offer of marriage?

The old familiar ache, no less sharp after all these years, sprang up inside her. How could she agree to such an arrange-ment? She'd spent enough time pining for a man too hung up on his career to give her the kind of love she needed.

Kael played second fiddle to no one. Not in the rodeo arena and not, she felt sure, in marriage. If she married him, she would lose control, over her life, her farm, her son, everything.

And nothing frightened Daisy more than the loss of control.

From the moment her parents had been killed, she'd

assumed the role as head of household. Cleanly, swiftly, without complaint, she'd abandoned her own hopes and dreams in favor of doing the right thing.

At sixteen she'd made funeral arrangements in the midst of running the honey farm. Daisy had gone to court and gotten declared an emancipated minor. She'd succeeded on sheer grit and hardheaded determination. Finishing high school at the top of her class while at the same time providing for her family.

It had been very difficult, but Daisy attained a level of emotional independence rarely achieved by someone so young. She was used to getting her own way, and that's how she liked it. She was used to being in charge and wasn't about to surrender her independence for any man.

Never mind that once upon a time, she would have given anything for him to ask her to be his wife. That time had long since passed. She wasn't about to go running back to him with open arms, no matter how bright the old flame burned within her.

*What about Travis?*

Indeed, what about her child? The boy deserved to know his father, and Kael, for all his faults, deserved a chance to prove himself. Not to her, but to his son.

"We don't have to get married for you to be a father," Daisy said. "You live right next door. That should be good enough."

Kael reached out and touched a lock of her hair, caressing it between his index finger and thumb. Daisy suppressed a shiver and cast her gaze to the floor.

"Maybe I want *more* than just being a father."

She inhaled sharply and took a step backward. "What do you mean?"

"I've missed you, Daisy." His voice was hoarse, husky, like he'd shouted too long and too hard. "More than you can ever know."

"Don't tell me you didn't have buckle bunnies chasing you around the circuit, because I know better, Kael." She said the first thing that came to her mind, anything to pick a fight and keep her anger smoldering.

"You're never going to let me live down my mistakes, are you?"

"It's a little hard when your biggest boo-boo is a six-year-old child."

"Which is why I want to make amends."

"You're forgetting one thing," Daisy said, her tone sharp-edged.

"What's that?"

"A marriage should be based on love."

"We used to love each other, once. Remember?" His fingers lingered on her shoulder, sending warm tingles over her skin. "We could try again. Get those feelings back."

Daisy shook her head. She didn't want to resurrect those old memories. She opened her mouth and told him a bald-faced lie. A fib designed to protect her heart and push him away. "That's where you're wrong, Kael. I was hot for you, yes, but it was just infatuation. What we had wasn't real love."

෯෫෯

DAISY ANNE WAS NOT A GOOD LIAR. THE TIP OF HER NOSE TURNED RED when she told a whopper, and right now the cute upturned tip was crimson.

Kael forced himself not to grin. No matter what she might claim, the woman still cared about him. Now how could he get her to see that they were, and always had been, meant for each other?

"Why would you want to marry someone who doesn't want you?" she asked.

"Because that someone is the adoptive mother of my child."

"Dang you, Kael," she said. "I regret the day I ever clamped eyes on you."

"I'm aware of that," he replied coolly. "Tell you what, Daisy, I'll give you a week to make up your mind. In the meantime, I'm ready to introduce myself to my son."

Daisy raised a hand to her mouth. "Can't we wait a little while longer? Ease Travis into the idea?"

"I don't think so. It's way past time."

"Don't you dare go against me on this, Kael! I'm not ready."

Kael reached down and picked his hat up off the floor from where it had fallen when he'd kissed her. "All right. We'll play it your way. I'll give you a week to think over my proposal. After that..." He shook his head. "I'll have to get my lawyer involved. And she's not going to go easy on a woman who has kept a man from his son for six years."

Kael thrust his chest out with more bravado than he felt. The woman was stubborn enough to call his bluff. If push came to shove, and she still refused to marry him? Well, Kael didn't have the heart to wreck her world, but he wasn't about to let her know that.

"You have changed," Daisy said quietly. "I was wrong before. Unfortunately, the change wasn't for the better."

Kael shrugged. "A man's gotta do what a man's gotta do." With those parting words, he turned and sauntered from the room, quietly struggling against the pain in his leg and trying his best not to limp.

***

"Bad news?" Aunt Peavy peered at Daisy through her thick glasses from where she stood at the kitchen sink, peeling apples for a homemade pie.

Three days had passed since Kael asked her to marry him. Three days of worrying, cursing, and pacing the floor. Three days of feeling like an animal caught in a trap with no way out save gnawing a paw off.

Daisy switched off her cell phone and sat down at the kitchen table. "Worse than that. The green monster has officially expired. Willie said it'd cost three thousand dollars to fix her, and the thing's not worth five hundred. Said best we could do is sell her for scrap."

"Oh, Lordy, no." Aunt Peavy sighed and laid a hand over her chest. "Not more problems! What are we going to do?"

For once, Daisy wanted to join her aunt in her overreaction to bad news. She suppressed the urge to lay her head on the table and bawl her eyes out. She'd been strong for so long, she didn't even know how to let down her guard and simply sob her sorrows away.

"Maybe you better call Kael and tell him you'll marry him."

"Aunt Peavy! That is not a solution."

"Well," her aunt said. "Do you have any better ideas?"

"I'll get a job."

"Doin' what? It's not like jobs are poppin' out all over everywhere in Rascal."

"I know." Daisy plowed her hands through her hair. "I was thinking about applying in Pecos."

"That's a forty-mile drive one way. Who's gonna take care of the farm while you're gone all day? And how will you get there with no car?"

"I don't know." Daisy sighed.

Aunt Peavy got quiet.

Daisy rose to her feet, went to the sink, and patted her aunt's arm. "Look, I'm sorry I'm discouraged. This thing with Kael's knocked me off my game."

"It's okay. I'm just worried."

"I know you are." Daisy gave her a hug. "Don't fret. I'll find a way like I always do."

*Like I always do.*

The phrase echoed in her head. For once, she'd like to rest her burden on someone else's shoulders. How nice it would be to have someone else take the reins for once.

*Someone like Kael?*

No! What on earth was she thinking? He was not the solution to all her problems. He was just an even bigger complication.

And yet some tiny part of her dared to hope. Dared to daydream about what could be if she just said "yes" to his proposal.

The back door banged closed, jerking Daisy from her thoughts. She looked up to see Travis standing in the entryway, tears streaming down his cheeks.

She flew from her chair to her son's side. "Honey, what's wrong?"

"The kids are sa-sa—" Travis sobbed so hard he hiccuped on the sentence. "Saying I can't go on the Cub Scout father-son fishing trip 'cause I don't have a dad."

Daisy enveloped him in her arms. Seeing him so upset wrenched her heart in two. "Shh." She patted his back. "Take a few deep breaths."

Travis obeyed, his heavy sigh sending a shudder through his little body. He swiped at his eyes with the back of his hand.

"Better?"

He nodded, but a forlorn expression clouded his face, letting Daisy know it was definitely not better.

"Who said you couldn't go on the Cub Scout fishing trip?"

Travis rolled the hem of his shirttail between his fingers and studied his boots. "Scott Kelly and Tommy Martin. They said only boys with daddies could go."

Daisy forced her teeth together, biting down on her anger. It wouldn't be the first time that kids had taunted him.

"How come everybody has a daddy but me?" Travis raised his hazel eyes and stared at her. Accusing eyes that looked just like Kael's.

*But you do have a daddy, you do, you do.*

Was she wrong, after all, for wanting to wait before letting Kael tell Travis the truth?

"How about if I go with you to the picnic," Daisy said, avoiding his question.

Travis shook his head. "No, it's gotta be a dad."

Daisy rocked back on her heels. Father-son picnic indeed. Didn't the people who organized these things realize what they were doing to children without fathers? You'd think in this day and age people would have gotten over such prejudices.

But Rascal was a small town, and folks prided themselves on their old-fashioned values. Nothing wrong with that, except when it made people closed-minded to other ways of being in the world.

"Maybe Kael could take you."

Travis gave her a dubious look. "He's not my dad."

Her spirits plummeted. It was painfully obvious Travis needed a father. She'd been aware of it for some time.

"He would be if your mama married him," Aunt Peavy said, putting in her two cents worth at exactly the wrong time.

Travis perked up, and a wide grin crossed his face. "You're gonna marry Kael?"

Daisy shot Aunt Peavy a withering glance. "Honey..."

"Oh, Mom, please, please." He pressed his palms together in a prayer. "Kael is so cool, and I want a dad real bad."

Shame blazed a path through her. She'd called Kael selfish when she was being the selfish one. Daisy had allowed her own feelings toward Kael to get in the way of what was best for Travis.

Every child deserved two parents. But Kael could be his father without Daisy having to marry him.

"Mom?" Travis laid his hand on her shoulder and peered at her. "Are you okay?"

Daisy blinked and stared back at the child who was as much a part of her as if he'd grown in her womb. For Travis, she would do anything.

Even if that meant marrying Kael.

❄ 8 ❧

"**M**ay I speak with you a moment?"

Kael glanced up from where he sat on a bench in the barn, sharpening his mother's kitchen knives for her. He was surprised to see Daisy standing in the doorway, the afternoon sun slanting her shadow across the hay-strewn floor.

"Sure," he replied, setting the whetstone aside. "Come on in."

She hesitated at the door like a puppy on a leash. Even from the distance of ten feet, he could smell her honey-flavored aroma—rich, amber, sweet. Slim-cut blue jeans hugged her narrow hips. She wore a gray oversize T-shirt that should have camouflaged her breasts instead of accentuating them as the shirt did.

Kael caught his breath and battled the feelings rising inside him. The woman tempted him more every day.

She kept her hands clasped behind her back and avoided meeting his gaze. "This isn't easy for me."

"What isn't easy?" Nonplussed, he cocked his head and

studied her. Her cheeks were pink, but the rest of her face was so pale her freckles stood out prominently.

"Saying what I've got to say."

He ignored the chugging sensation in his belly and patted the bench beside him. "Have a seat."

"I'd rather stand."

Kael shrugged. "Suit yourself."

She twisted her fingers into an anxious knot and bounced on the balls of her feet. "I've reconsidered."

He froze, not quite certain he'd heard her correctly, barely daring to hope. More than anything in the world, he wanted to marry Daisy and be a proper father to his son.

She cleared her throat.

"Reconsidered what?" he asked, feeling as if he were gingerly stepping over invisible land mines.

"You know."

"Tell me, Daisy. Say the words."

She let out her breath, stuffed her hands in her pockets, and made it a point to stare at the horse stalls along the back wall. "Your offer. I've reconsidered."

"What offer is that?" It wasn't kind of him, but he couldn't resist baiting her. Kael experienced a fluttering sensation inside his chest. What had happened to cause this change of heart? Whatever the cause, he was grateful.

"Why do you have to be so difficult?" She rolled her eyes.

"It's not often I see the proud Daisy Hightower grovel, and I gotta admit I'm enjoying it." Kael folded his arms across his chest and grinned.

"Oh, forget it. I should have known you'd be a jerk." Daisy spun on her heels.

"Whoa!" Kael leaped up, all smugness gone, and dashed across the floor to grab her arm before she got away. "Wait. I'm sorry."

She twisted in his grasp, her skin hot beneath his fingers. Kael gulped but held on.

"I'm sorry," he repeated.

He felt her muscles relax. She tossed her head and sliced him a saucy expression. A look that made him want her all the more.

"Shall we start over?" He raised an eyebrow, worried now that his teasing had made her change her mind.

"All right."

"You've come to accept my marriage proposal?" His heart beat faster.

She nodded. "Yes, but I want it understood this is strictly a marriage of convenience. I'm agreeing to this arrangement for Travis' sake and because I desperately need help around the farm. Plus, the green monster died."

"You don't have to marry me to get a vehicle, Daisy. My parents have several old farm trucks. We could sell you a pickup and you could pay it out."

"I'll take you up on that offer," she said, looking relieved. "But this is more than that. I'm thinking of Travis' future."

He studied her face, searching for the smallest sign of emotion. A twitch of her eye, an upturned smile, anything that would tell him she still had feelings for him. But Daisy had schooled her emotions for too many years. Kael could read nothing from her expression.

"I can appreciate where you're coming from."

"You'd better. I'm marrying you for your money and for my son. Those are the only reasons."

"So you said." Kael narrowed his eyes. He didn't want her to know she'd just ripped his heart from his chest.

"You seem awfully accepting about this."

"I want us to be a family. That's all that matters."

Daisy wrinkled her nose in frustration. "You do understand what a marriage in name only means, don't you?"

"What are you getting at?" He leaned closer, and she took a step backward.

"There'll be no consummation of the marriage vows."

"You mean you won't make love to me."

"That's correct." She held her head high, her shoulders straight and her lips pressed into an unyielding line, but despite her hardline stance, Kael knew he wasn't imagining the red flush creeping up her neck. Daisy was embarrassed.

Kael stuck his tongue against his cheek to keep from grinning. It had taken a lot for her to come to him and accept his proposal. He knew exactly how much pride it had cost her, and he wondered what caused her abrupt change of heart.

"Well?" she demanded, drawing herself up to her full five foot four inches. "Is it a deal?"

"Marriage in name only?" Kael fingered his jaw. "You're asking a lot from a red-blooded male. You expect me to spend the rest of my life without sex?"

The pink blush on her face darkened to brilliant scarlet. "I...I...er," she stammered.

Her hesitancy told him she hadn't given the issue much thought from his viewpoint. Suddenly, without knowing how he knew Kael realized Daisy was still a virgin. A soft, melting sensation stirred inside his chest.

A knot of emotion lodged in his throat, surprising Kael with its intensity. He had an irresistible yearning to swing her into his arms, bury his face in her hair, and tell her exactly how much he loved her. But Kael was terrified of scaring her away.

"Well?" He arched an eyebrow.

"You can have your own...er...private life."

"You're giving me permission to sleep with other women?"

"Since it won't be a real marriage in the carnal sense of the word, then you're free to do what you like in that area, yes."

He noticed Daisy's breathing was ragged, her pupils dilated. He wanted to tell her that no other woman on the face of the earth could ever tempt him to break his wedding vows to her, but something held his tongue. Because of what had happened with Rose, Daisy still did not trust him. No matter what he might say, he could only prove himself over time.

"What about you?" he asked. "What about your needs?"

"I'm too busy for needs."

"So, you'll go the rest of your life without sex?"

She shrugged. "If it's necessary."

He wanted to tell her she could take lovers as well, but dammit, he could not get the words out of his mouth. He did not want a marriage in name only. But he surprised himself by saying, "All right."

"You agree?" her voice came out high and squeaky.

"Yes."

"That's good then." She stuffed her hands in her back pockets and nodded her head, but she looked unhappy.

"So, no lovemaking between us?" he ventured.

"None."

"Never?"

"Ever," she replied firmly.

"If that's the way it's gotta be." Kael shrugged like he didn't care, but once they were actually married, however, all bets were off. By hook or by crook, she was going to be his bride. In *every* sense of the word. He would win her over. No matter how long it took.

"That leaves one other provision."

"Let's hear it." Kael waved an expansive hand.

"We don't tell Travis you're his biological father."

"Wait a minute, I can't agree to that."

"Please let me finish." Daisy frowned. "We won't tell him for now."

Kael shook his head. "No. I don't like this. Why wait?"

"I think he needs time to get used to the idea of having a man about the house."

"Why can't that man be his father?"

"You're a stranger."

"I won't be for long."

"He's only six years old," Daisy argued. "He won't understand the complexities of his conception."

"We don't have to tell him *that.*"

"What are you going to tell him when he asks why you waited six years to come back into his life?"

Twisting his face in thought, Kael paused to consider her wisdom. "When would we tell him?"

"When the time is right."

Kael mulled that over. He saw no value in waiting, but Daisy was the boy's mother. She knew Travis better than he did. Still, it would be hard not telling his son the truth.

"Besides," Daisy said, reeling in a heavy sigh.

"Besides what?"

"We really don't know how long you'll be able to stick with this marriage. If you get tired and wanderlust hits, it'll be easier for Travis to accept you leaving if he doesn't know you're his real father."

"Do you really believe I'd walk out on you?"

"You did it before."

"No, Daisy, that's not true. Back then, we had not committed ourselves to each other. This time it's different. This time it's for keeps. I have no doubts about my own serious intentions. What I want to know is, are *you* up to the challenge?"

❦

THREE DAYS LATER, DAISY AND KAEL STOOD BEFORE THE JUSTICE OF the peace at the Presidio County Courthouse with Travis and Aunt Peavy, and their neighbors, Keegan Wren Winslow in attendance. Kael's parents were in New York City on business and hadn't been able to come.

It was just as well, Daisy decided. She was nervous enough going ahead with this marriage without all the normal wedding fanfare.

Kael had bought her a bouquet of pink roses, red carnations, and white baby's breath. Also, he'd given her with one of the Carmody ranch trucks. A western hauler with room to transport her hives. The pickup might be old in Kael's book, but the truck was the newest vehicle she'd ever owned, and he insisted it was a wedding present.

Although she'd protested both the flowers and the truck as a gift, the gesture touched her. Kael seemed serious about the whole marriage thing.

At least for now, she reminded herself. Anybody could stay in one place for a few months. What happened when those months turned into years, and the years turned to decades? Would Kael remain at her side or would he quickly grow bored in Rascal and leave her? And if by some miracle he did stay longer, what would happen in twelve years when Travis graduated high school and there was no longer a reason for them to stay married?

Daisy swallowed hard and pushed those disturbing thoughts aside. Smoothing imaginary wrinkles from her cream-colored linen suit, Daisy shifted her weight and focused her gaze on Judge Crinshaw.

Sensing her uneasiness, Kael reached over and squeezed her hand.

She darted a glance at him and found him smiling tenderly. That smile was almost her undoing. Daisy's knees knocked together, and perspiration trickled down the hollow of her throat.

Years ago, when she used to imagine their wedding, she had pictured something entirely different. Like every other girl who'd dreamed the dream, she'd envisioned the most stunning dress of white lace and satin with a mesh veil and a long train. She'd foreseen the ceremony in a church and a dinner reception to follow. She'd pictured scads of guests, a lot of wedding presents, a large diamond engagement ring, and a honeymoon trip to Hawaii.

A fairy tale.

She was getting none of those things. Neither was she getting the most important thing of all—unconditional love.

Her lip trembled as tears built behind her eyelids. Too late for any of that. She had to settle for what she had and hope against all hope that somehow, some way Kael would come to love her as much as she loved him. If that never happened, she could take comfort in the knowledge she'd provided a father for her son.

"Daisy?" Judge Crinshaw's voice cut through her thoughts.

She blinked. "Yes?"

"Repeat after me."

Numbly, she parroted her wedding vows back to the judge. Kael clung fast to her hand, but she didn't dare look at him for fear her tears would break loose and tumble down her cheeks for everyone to see.

Everyone, being the judge, Aunt Peavy, Travis, Keegan and Wren.

"Do you, Daisy Anne Hightower, take Kael Jacob Carmody to be your lawfully wedded husband?"

"I do," she murmured.

"And do you, Kael Jacob Carmody, take Daisy Anne Hightower to be your lawfully wedded wife?"

"I do." His voice rang loud and true.

"By the power vested in me by the state of Texas, I now pronounce you man and wife."

That was it. In seven minutes, they were married, and the ceremony was over. Hitched. United, tied together, joined as one. Until death do they part, or until Kael decided he was bored with the role of husband and father.

"You may kiss the bride."

LORI WILDE

Daisy turned to face the music, her bouquet shaking crazily in her hands.

Kael rested both hands on her shoulders. He stared intently into her eyes.

She felt herself falling deeper, harder, faster into the vortex of Kael's gaze. Holding her breath, her heart skipped.

He leaned in close and gently kissed her.

Aunt Peavy applauded. Judge Crinshaw congratulated them. Keegan and Wren gave them hugs and wished them a marriage as happy as their own.

Travis grinned from ear to ear. "I got me a dad."

"Yes, you do, and I'm delighted to have such a fine young man for a son," Kael said.

Kael's eyes shone brightly, and Daisy could have sworn the man was close to tears. Looking from her new husband to her child, Daisy knew she had made the correct decision. Travis' happiness meant far more than her own.

"Now we can go on the Cub Scout fishing trip!"

"And that's just for starters." Kael tousled the boy's hair. "There'll be marshmallow roasts and swimming and camping."

"Wow." Travis' eyes lit up.

Judge Crinshaw smiled. "I wish you folks the very best. I can tell you're going to make a great family." He shook their hands.

Guilt gnawed at Daisy. Unwittingly, the judge had just married them under false pretenses. He assumed they were truly in love and planning a real life together. A hollow ache, worse than the pain she'd experienced when Kael had left Rascal to join the rodeo circuit, sank into her stomach.

"Daisy." Kael held his arm to her.

Hesitantly, she accepted his hand. His grip was warm, strong, and reassuring, and she was surprised at the comfort she drew from him.

They walked from the room, Travis and Aunt Peavy following behind. Keegan and Wren waved goodbye and headed to their vehicle. Aunt Peavy's hands fluttered in the air like an excitable bird, and she talked fast without hardly taking a breath.

Outside they paused on the courthouse steps and squinted against the bright noonday sun. Daisy felt odd, as if she were an actress playing the role of dutiful bride.

"I never thought I'd live to see the day," Aunt Peavy exclaimed with a contented sigh. "Our Daisy finally married."

"Guess this means you're officially my aunt now too," Kael said.

"Oh, yes, please think of me like that, my boy."

"Come here, Auntie." Kael dropped Daisy's hand and enveloped Aunt Peavy in a bear hug.

She giggled like a teenager. "Listen," Aunt Peavy said, pulling away and digging in her purse for a handful of twenties. "I want to do something special for you two. How 'bout I pay for your honeymoon night in that fancy hotel in Marfa?"

"Why, Aunt Peavy," Kael said, "that's a sweet gesture."

"No," Daisy said, "it's too much."

Kael and Aunt Peavy both stared at her.

"Goodness' sakes, child, let me do something nice for you for once," Aunt Peavy chided.

Daisy shook her head. "There's not going to be a honeymoon."

Disappointment etched Aunt Peavy's kind face. "No honeymoon?"

Kael cocked his eyebrow. "Daisy, it's rude to refuse a gift."

Yeah. Just what she wanted, a night alone with Kael in some romantic honeymoon suite. Who knew what ulterior motives lurked up his sleeve? Well, she was having none of it. They had an agreement. This marriage was in name only.

"There's too much work to be done on the farm. I don't have time for frivolous things like a honeymoon." Then, before Aunt Peavy or Kael could protest, Daisy took Travis' hand and started across the street to where Kael's pickup truck was parked.

"That's right, Miss High-and-Mighty," she heard Kael mumble. "Keep your guard up. Don't dare let anyone get close enough to care about you."

Bristling, Daisy halted in the middle of the street and turned around to glare at Kael. "I tried trusting someone once. Remember?" She looked down at her son. "We both know how *that* turned out."

"Daisy." Kael stalked over to grab her elbow in a viselike grip. "Get out of the street."

A car horn blared.

"Oh, my. Oh, my," Aunt Peavy exclaimed, still perched on the courthouse lawn. "Somebody's gonna get run over."

"Mom," Travis said, his eyebrows bunched together in a worried expression. "Are you and my new daddy having a fight?"

"No, Travis, we're not having a fight," Kael said. He ushered Daisy and Travis to the curb before going back across the street to collect Aunt Peavy.

All resistance left Daisy's body. She had to start controlling her responses to Kael, especially in front of Travis. She shouldn't allow the man to affect her the way he did.

Travis and Aunt Peavy chattered on the way home, relieving Daisy of carrying on a conversation with Kael. For that, she was grateful. She sat quietly, seat belt girded around her lap, the bridal bouquet clutched in her lap.

An inexplicable sadness settled over her.

This was her wedding day. She should be deliriously happy. Instead, the future loomed murky and uncertain. How long could this last? When would he grow tired of his impersonation of husband and father and hit the road? Worst of all, how long before Kael eroded her defenses, and she allowed him into her bed?

Daisy bit down on her knuckle at the thought. She peeked over to see Kael. The scent of roses and carnations hung in the air, reminding her of what had just taken place. A wedding. Like it or not, the three of them were now a family. She had to find some way of coming to terms with that.

"Daisy?"

She raised her head. Kael dangled the truck keys from his finger. His tone was kind, tender and touched her more than she dared to admit.

"Huh?"

"We're home."

## 9

**H**ome.

She glanced around to see they were indeed back at the farm. "Oh."

Aunt Peavy and Travis had already gotten out of the vehicle and were making their way inside. Panic washed through her.

They were alone. Together. She and Kael. Mr. and Mrs. Carmody.

"Let's take a walk," Kael suggested.

"I don't want to."

"We need to talk."

There was a pleading in his eyes she'd never seen before. Despite her resolve, she felt her heart thaw.

"Okay," she acquiesced, letting him help her out of the truck. His touch, as always, was disorienting. He looped his elbow through hers and guided her down the driveway toward the honey house.

"You're still angry with me," he said, the spring breeze lightly ruffling his hair as they walked. His tangy cologne mixed with the smell of honeysuckle growing along the fence row and teased her nostrils.

"I don't know if angry is the right word—"

"You've never forgiven me for what happened."

"I haven't," she said, the old familiar hurt stabbing her fresh and new. "I don't know if I can."

"It was a long time ago, and I'm sorry for all the suffering I put you through. It wasn't my intention to hurt you, but I did."

She looked into his face. Gone was the cocky, self-assured Kael of old. The man walking beside her was contrite, apologetic.

"It's not something I can turn on and off like a switch."

"You can't hold a grudge for the rest of my life, Daisy. You're only hurting yourself in the long run."

"How do you figure?"

"You're turning bitter. Is that the way you want to spend your life?"

His words hit her hard. They were too true. Daisy ducked her chin and stared down at the dry, yellowed grass. She had been so hurt, she'd built a wall around her feelings. He was right. She did not want to spend her life angry and bitter.

"Haven't I paid enough for my sins? I've missed out on six years of my son's life," Kael went on.

"I did agree to marry you. That's a start, isn't it?" She pointed out, eager to show him she wasn't hopeless.

He stopped walking and cupped her hand in both of his. "Then let's make this a true marriage, Daisy. Let's try to make it work. For the sake of our son. He needs parents pulling together to make a real family. Can you do that?"

"What do you mean by a 'true marriage'?" She raised her chin and bravely met his gaze head on; her pulse galloped.

"I mean a marriage in every sense of the word."

"I'm sorry, Kael, I don't think I can give you what you're asking."

"Why is that? Because you're afraid to be loved, both emotionally and physically?"

"I'm not afraid," Daisy denied, but her voice warbled.

"I think you are."

"Since when did you become an expert on my feelings?"

"Since the first time I kissed you."

"Ha." Oh no, she was doing it again. Sounding bitter.

"Scoff if you will, but you hold your true emotions in check on purpose. You get mad to

hide the fact you're terrified of life."

"Me? Terrified of life? Who's the one who stayed here and assumed responsibility for your son? Who ran off to play cowboy?"

"Stop playing the martyr, Daisy. It's been your favorite part to play, but the reality is you threw yourself into hard work to keep from facing the truth. You stayed, but it's because you were too scared to do anything else. Too scared to even make love to me. That's why you don't want me in your bed. Not because you're mad, but because you're just plain chicken."

"That's not true," she denied, but deep inside she feared he was right.

"Is it? Then explain why you're still a virgin at twenty-six when most women are married with children. You've made it clear enough it isn't because you've been pining away for me."

Her face flamed hot. How had he known? Mortified that he'd guessed her secret, Daisy tried to pull away from him, but Kael clung tighter to her hand.

"No, ma'am," he said sharply, "you're not storming off. You're going to stay here until we hash this out."

"Please let me go," she whispered.

"Daisy, it's okay to be scared. All you have to do is admit it. You don't have to hide anything from me, sweetheart."

"Please don't call me that." Even her tone sounded panicky.

"Why not? You're my wife." He stroked her arm and sent goose bumps fleeing down her spine. "A man's supposed to say nice things to his wife."

*Wife.*

The word should have pleasant, happy connotations; instead, it felt like a noose. Tight and getting tighter, the higher his hand caressed.

No. She wasn't ready. Wasn't prepared to assume this new role.

"Please," she said again, "I can't."

"Can't or won't?"

She jerked away from him, and this time Kael let her go. Daisy turned and ran as fast as she could, the truth hitting her like a hammer. *Face it, deep down inside, you're a coward.*

SEVERAL WEEKS PASSED AFTER THEIR WEDDING DAY.

Kael spent most of his spare time with Travis. They attended the father-son Cub Scout fishing trip and had a blast. They built a campfire and roasted marshmallows, skipped stones over the stock pond, and rode horses. They played catch in the backyard, went to the movie matinee on Saturdays, and attended church services on Sunday mornings. Like a water-starved plant, the boy soaked up Kael's attention.

To Kael's surprise, he felt none of the negative emotions he'd once associated with parenthood. He never felt burdened or crowded or trapped. Desperate to make up for those lost years, each minute with his son was precious, even when they did nothing more than watch television together.

Travis asked a million questions about his life on the rodeo circuit. While Kael was thrilled to talk about his adventures to the boy, he was not in the least inclined to return to the life that was so quickly fading into the background.

Why had he resisted settling down for so long? Why had he ever imagined that fatherhood would be a death knell to his own youth? What had he been looking for on the rodeo circuit, that he couldn't get right here in Rascal?

Kael puzzled over the questions. The happiness bull riding had brought to him paled in comparison to having a son.

Except for his relationship with Daisy, life had never been so enriching.

Daisy, however, was another story. Things between them remained strained, and he didn't know how to reach her.

During the day they worked side by side reorganizing the depleted hives. But she could go for hours without talking. When he tried to make light conversation, she answered him in mono-syllables. Eventually he gave up trying to get her attention and concentrated on strengthening the bond between himself and Travis.

She'll come around, he assured himself, but deep down inside, he was beginning to wonder.

In truth, he loved her more now than ever. Watching her in work brought him to understand exactly what she'd sacrificed for his son over the years.

If only there were some way to break through the barrier that she'd erected around herself and her emotions. For Kael knew that underneath that hard outer shell lay the most tender of hearts. A heart so vulnerable, so fragile she refused to allow anyone near for fear of getting hurt again.

And he'd been the cause of so much of her pain.

That knowledge was the one thing that kept him holding on, clinging to the hope that one day Daisy would give her love free rein, forgive him his sins, and welcome him back home with open arms. Until then, he could do nothing but give her space and wait.

At night Kael slept in the spare bedroom, fighting growing thoughts of how things could be between them. Torturing himself with visions of Daisy, her dark-red hair flowing freely down her back, her slender, well-built body encased in a thin, white cotton nightgown, he imagined her

slipping into his room at midnight, her pent-up passion, so hot and deep, spilling over him in erotic waves. He pictured them making love on the cool, crisp sheets, their bodies joined, their perspiration mingled.

In the end, he was only driving himself crazy because Daisy showed no signs of giving in. He tried every tactic—kind words, thoughtful gifts, generous gestures. He ran bathwater for Travis. He cooked breakfast. He washed dishes. Trying to show her this parenthood thing was a team effort. She would thank him, then go about her business.

Kael racked his brain, striving for some way to crack her brick wall and make her take a second look at him. Finally, three weeks after their marriage, he simply decided to leave her to her own devices.

"We need to recolonize the eight hives near the stock pond," Daisy announced one Saturday morning. Kael and Travis sat on the couch, still in their pajamas, eating sugar-frosted cornflakes and watching the Cartoon Network. "Boss Martin at the feed store called to say the new queens have arrived. I'm going to pick them up." She stared at them, a gleam of envy in her eyes.

*She's feeling left out*, Kael thought.

"I'll be back in half an hour, and I hope to see you both dressed and off the couch." She twirled the truck keys on her finger.

"Aw, Mom," Travis complained.

"Don't 'aw, Mom' me," she scolded. "You have chores."

"Daisy don't be such a grouch," Kael coaxed. "Relax, it's Saturday morning."

"The bees don't know what day of the week it is," she said. "I've got a lot of work to do."

She seemed sad and lonely. Kael ached to reach out to her

and draw her into the circle of his arms, but the firm set to her shoulders warned him off. *Oh, Daisy, if you'd only let yourself, you could be curled up with us, too!*

Without a backward glance, she scooped up her purse from the wing chair and left the room. Kael winced, put his empty cereal bowl on the coffee table, and ran a hand down his face.

Could Daisy's heart ever be repaired? Had he ruined her loving spirit when he'd inadvertently slept with Rose?

*Daisy, Daisy, Daisy, how can I reach you?* Kael fretted. The answer floated to him, simple and true.

*Tell her you love her.*

He hadn't told her he loved her before now because he feared she wouldn't believe him. For Daisy, words weren't enough. She had to be shown. When she came to accept that he wasn't going to leave, then she'd start to trust him.

What if she never did?

That idea, glaring in its possibility, wrenched his gut. No. He refused to give up. He'd keep at her until she understood how much he loved her.

"Come on, sport," Kael said, affectionately ruffling Travis' hair. "Let's make your mom happy." He picked up the remote control and snapped off the television set.

"Okay." Travis sprang off the couch. "Maybe we can go outside and fly my Batman kite before she gets home."

Kael glanced out the window. "I don't know if it's windy enough."

"Please?" Travis turned his hazel eyes on Kael and melted him instantly.

"Okay, champ, we'll give it a shot." Kael clapped his hands. "Now, let's get rolling."

DRIVING BACK FROM THE FEED STORE, A DOZEN BOXES OF CAGED

queen bees wedged securely in the bed of Kael's pickup truck, Daisy mentally scolded herself for her sour attitude. Since her marriage to Kael, she'd been on edge.

She hated being this way. She wanted to laugh and smile and have a good time. But she was scared. Terrified that if she let down her guard Kael would break her heart all over again.

Even if Kael was kidding himself that he could be the perfect father, she knew better. Eventually he'd grow tired of the demands of family responsibilities. Eventually his old restlessness would rear its ugly head. Eventually the glamorous lure of the rodeo would have him shuffling on down the road.

Oh sure, for now he was pulling out all the stops, making the grand gesture of playing proud papa, but Daisy knew that could not last. The picnics, the ball games, the horseback rides would come to a screeching halt once the novelty of having a son wore off and the reality of parenthood set in.

Wait until Kael discovered what it was like to nurse a sick kid through the night or get a call from the school principal concerning a discipline problem or spend tedious hours helping with homework.

*What's the matter, Daisy, jealous?*

The thought, like a sharp jolt from the devil's pitchfork, prodded her.

"That's ridiculous," Daisy muttered under her breath. "I'm not jealous of Kael."

But she had to admit it irked her that he'd wheedled his way into Travis' heart so easily. They'd formed an instant rapport that sometimes left Daisy feeling like the bad guy when she had to enforce bedtime hours or deny Travis the sweet desserts Kael brought home. Sure, it was easy for Kael. He got to be the hero.

Sighing, Daisy turned into the driveway. She killed the pickup's engine, got out, and went inside to find Aunt Peavy making chicken soup and a tossed green salad for lunch.

"Hi," Daisy greeted her. "How was choir practice?"

"Not too bad. Though somebody should tell Myrtle Higgins that she can't sing. 'Course Reverend Hobson is not about to say a word to the poor old soul."

Daisy cloaked a smile. Three-fourths of the ladies in the church choir, Aunt Peavy included, sang off-key.

"Where's Kael and Travis?" Daisy asked. "Not still in front of the television set, I hope."

Aunt Peavy shrugged. "I dunno. They were gone when Jenny dropped me off."

"Hmm, where did they get off to?"

"Jenny will be back for me around six. We're rehearsing all evening for the passion play on Sunday, so Jenny just invited me to spend the night with her. Is that okay with you?"

"Sure." Daisy spied a note stuck to the refrigerator with a Cookie Monster magnet. She plucked the piece of paper off the door and read what Kael had written: *Daisy, we're already at the pond. Love, K and T."*

Love?

Her pulse quickened.

*Don't read anything into it. It's just something people put in a letter.*

What were they doing at the pond? Daisy hoped this didn't mean that Kael and Travis were attempting to handle the bees on their own without her supervision. Kael knew little about beekeeping and although Travis was familiar with the procedures, he was still a little boy.

Frowning, she fidgeted with her wedding ring. She still hadn't gotten used to the weight of it on her finger. Just as she hadn't yet gotten used to sharing her life and her son.

*Why had he taken the boy off without waiting for her?*

Darn him.

A calm, peaceful voice whispered in the back of her head. *Don't be so contrary, Daisy.*

Willing herself into a more positive frame of mind, Daisy went back outside, opened the gate

to the back pasture, then drove the truck through the field. The vehicle bumped and swayed over the rutted dirt road leading to the stock pond located at the farm's back perimeter.

Something in the sky caught her attention, and she raised her eyes to the clouds. A black Batman kite dipped and bobbed. Relief washed over her. Kael and Travis weren't messing with the bees; they were flying a kite.

She rounded a clump of oak trees flanking the stock pond on the left. To the right lay the eight beehives she'd positioned near the wildflowers growing along the top of the pond. This time of the year, only sunflowers remained, the bluebonnets, black-eyed Susan, and paintbrushes had disappeared for the season.

Travis was running fast, trying to urge the kite higher. Kael stood a few yards away, hands on his hips and a bright smile on his face as he watched their son.

*Their* son.

Even though they had not conceived this boy together, Travis was their son, and they had joined themselves in matrimony in order to provide for him. Though she didn't believe for one minute that the marriage would last, she had to admit it had taken a lot of guts on Kael's part to take such a life-changing step, even temporarily.

Travis had turned and was running backward, his eyes glued to the kite rising in the sky.

"Travis! Watch where you're going!" Kael shouted.

But his warning came too late. Before Travis could react, the boy plowed headlong into a beehive.

The hive teetered precariously on one leg, then tumbled over, bees rushing from the top in an angry, swarming horde.

"Oh, no!" Daisy gasped.

She slammed on the brakes, threw the truck into park, and frantically grabbed for the bee smoker resting on the floorboard.

But Kael was closer and quicker. By the time she freed herself from the seat belt and stumbled from the truck, he'd darted across the ground, scooped Travis into his arm, and fled for the stock pond, a thick swarm of black bees bearing down on them.

Kael limped as he ran, but he didn't let the injury slow him down.

Daisy's heart knocked against her rib cage. Her mouth went dry at the same time her palms turned slick with sweat and fear whipped her stomach.

"Run! Run!" she cried, fumbling in her pocket for a match and trying to strike it as she hurried toward the bees.

Kael held Travis tight against his chest and bent his body low over the boy's. The water's salvation lay several feet away, the bees just inches from descending upon them. She could hear their enraged hum even at this distance. A cold chill chased up her spine, and she swallowed past the lump lodged in her throat.

She was forced to stop long enough to light the newspaper in the smoker, her fingers bumbling with match after match.

Kael stumbled against Travis' weight, and his boot hung on a cactus. He floundered to keep his balance.

The bees swooped.

Daisy shrieked.

Gathering Travis into a ball, Kael hurled the boy forward to safety in the stock pond at the same time he came down on his bad leg, twisting it beneath him.

Travis disappeared into the pond, water splashing in his wake.

The bees converged upon the only remaining target.

*Kael.*

He covered his head with his hands, but the bees were relentless. They descended upon him in attack.

The smoker caught fire at last, and Daisy's legs churned as she ran, but it felt as if she were slogging through mud.

"Oh, Kael, oh, Kael, oh, Kael," she chanted, mentally wincing against the pain she knew he was suffering.

After what seemed like an eternity, she reached his side, pumping the bellow of the smoker over Kael's inert body, desperately battling back the bees.

With a sweeping gesture, she brushed at the bees, shoving them from his head and face with one hand while she pumped the bellows with the other. Smoke filled her nostrils, and she coughed against the acrid taste burning her throat.

Staring at Kael's still form, tears stung her eyes. She told herself it was the effects of the smoke, but that wasn't the case. Truth was, she felt as if her own skin was alive with bee stings.

"Kael!" she cried, "can you speak?"

He groaned.

Tears ran down Daisy's cheek and splashed onto Kael's hair. The back of his hands—still locked tight against his head—were covered in ugly red welts. The side of his face had also taken a bad hit. His flesh was a brilliant pink and swelling rapidly.

Daisy pumped the bellows around Kael, smothering him in smoke. His chest heaved. Daisy hissed in her breath. She had to get him to the house and poke some antihistamines down him before the reaction to the beestings worsened.

"Are you allergic to bees?" she asked, praying he was not. If he was allergic, they wouldn't make it to the hospital in time. He hadn't been allergic before, but you could develop an allergy at any time.

He shook his head and croaked, "No."

Lulled and disoriented, the bees lost their thirst for revenge and gradually flew back to circle the overturned hive.

"Can you walk?" Daisy pushed a bedraggled strand of hair from her face.

Kael groaned again and struggled to sit up.

Daisy's heart lurched.

"My knee," he replied.

"Here, brace yourself against me." She squatted next to him and offered her shoulder for support.

He draped his arms around her neck.

"On the count of three, we both stand up," she instructed. "One."

He positioned his foot in the dirt. Daisy looked down, unable to look what the beestings had done to his skin. His eyes were puffy, his cheeks misshapen, his swollen lip protruding.

"Two."

He nodded his readiness.

"Three."

They rose in unison, Kael grunting against the pain and favoring his bad knee.

"There," Daisy said matter-of-factly, dusting him off with her hands. Except, standing here with the man who'd just sacrificed himself to save their son from angry bees, had her feeling anything but matter-of-fact.

Kael squinted at her through the slits that were now his eyes. "Where's Travis? Is he okay?"

Daisy swiveled her head and saw Travis soaking wet and trembling behind them.

"Mom?" he whispered tentatively, his shirt plastered against his thin frame.

"Are you okay, son?"

He nodded. "Not even one sting, thanks to Dad."

*Dad.*

She'd never heard Travis call Kael that before. Daisy gulped and swung her gaze back to Kael. Had he gone against her wishes and told Travis the truth? She bit down on her lip. Now was certainly not the time to ask.

Kael managed a smile in his son's direction. "Anytime, champ."

Tears sprang into Travis' eyes. "I'm sorry I knocked over the hive."

"Could've happened to anyone," Kael said.

"That's right," Daisy soothed, gently patting their son on the shoulder. "Kael's going to be fine." Daisy turned to Kael. "We've got to get you back to the house. The swelling's getting worse. Can you walk?"

"Yeah," Kael said, his throat dry and scratchy. "Let's go."

## ☙ 10 ❧

Gingerly, Daisy guided Kael toward the truck, while Travis brought up the rear. Kael kept a firm grip on her arm, and Daisy realized for the first time in their relationship, he truly needed her.

Instantly, she was overwhelmed by a rush of blind love pumping furiously through her for this man who had somehow become her husband.

Daisy put Kael in bed and dosed him with a round of antihistamines and analgesics. She used her fingernails to scrape the stingers left in his skin, counting twenty-seven stingers.

But he had more stings where the stingers had not embedded into his skin. She'd count them all later. She applied cool compresses to his face, neck, and the back of his head. She also placed an ice pack on his swollen knee.

"That feels good," Kael murmured, lying back against the pillows, his eyes closed.

Perching on the edge of the mattress beside him, Daisy battled strong emotions. Emotions like forgiveness, remorse, and abiding love.

He'd rescued their child. Placing himself in harm's way. That selfless act went a long way in her estimation. Maybe Kael's bull riding accident had changed him.

She resisted the urge to trace her fingers along his arm. The bud of desire she'd suppressed for so long sprouted inside her like a fresh, green shoot reaching hungrily for the sun. Kael's vulnerability strummed a resonant chord in her soul that had been silent for too long.

"I'll let you sleep." Daisy cupped her hand to her chest and inched backward from the room. "And check in on you later."

Drowsily, Kael barely nodded, the antihistamines already kicking in.

Ignoring her thumping heart, Daisy turned and fled, pulling the bedroom door closed behind her.

Aunt Peavy stood in the hallway, her arms folded over her ample bosom, a concerned expression twisting her lips downward. "How's he doing?"

"Sore, but he'll be okay in a few hours. Thank God, he's not allergic to bee stings."

Aunt Peavy made a hissing sound as she sucked air around her dentures. "He sure looked terrible when you dragged him in here."

"I counted fifty-five stings in total. Some with stingers embedded, some not." Daisy shook her head, knowing from experience the pain he was feeling.

"That'd take the starch out of anybody's sail, even someone as tough as Kael."

"He'll be okay, but he's miserable."

"You better go have a talk with Travis. He's beside himself with worry. Thinks it's all his fault. He even refused my chocolate chip cookies."

"I'll speak to him." Daisy walked past Aunt Peavy to find Travis in the kitchen, his face buried in his hands, his head resting on the table, his shoulders moving silently as he sobbed.

"Honey." Daisy sat down beside him and gently patted his hair. He was still wet from the pond. "Kael's going to be all right."

Travis raised his head. "I did it." He hiccuped, tears matting on his eyelashes. "It's all my fault. Dad told me to stay away from the hives, but I wasn't payin' no attention."

*Dad.*

That word again. She loved that Travis was getting close to Kael, but it also worried her. Did Kael have what it took to stick around? The more Travis got attached to him, the harder it would be on the boy if wanderlust hit and Kael took off again.

"Shh." She leaned over and cradled Travis to her chest. "It's okay. Kael doesn't blame you. Accidents happen."

Travis wiped at his eyes. "Are you sure?"

"Positive. Now give me a kiss."

He gulped, swiped at his eyes, and kissed her cheek.

"That's my boy." She smiled. "Now get out of these wet clothes and take a bath. I've got to go see about that righting that hive."

"Okay, Mom." He managed a wan grin. "And thanks."

"What for?"

"For not getting mad at us for flying the kite and knocking over the hive."

"Sweetie, why would I get mad?"

Travis shrugged and avoided her gaze. "I dunno. Ever since you married Kael, you've been kinda gripey."

His statement, painful but accurate, startled Daisy. Had her marriage to Kael affected her personality? She needed to do some serious soul searching. Perhaps she'd been judging her new husband too harshly.

"I'm sorry if I've been out of sorts lately. I guess I'm just worried about the bees. Will you forgive me?"

"Sure." His grin returned, brighter this time, and in that split-second he looked exactly like Kael.

"Run on upstairs and get that bath." She gave him a hug. "I'll see you after a while."

Daisy watched her son go, a myriad of emotions darting through her. It was clear she had to change her attitude. If not, the barrier she'd built around her heart would eventually extend to her child. She couldn't allow that to happen. Resolving to be a better person, Daisy gathered her beekeeping equipment and headed back to the field.

She spent the rest of the afternoon restoring the overturned hive and dequeening the remaining colonies near the pond. No matter how hard she worked, she couldn't erase Travis' comment from her mind.

She had to start acting more positive toward his father. She had to give him a chance to prove he'd changed. For her son's sake, if not her own.

By late afternoon, when she'd completed her chores, Daisy's mind was made up. She'd have a heart-to-heart talk with Kael and tell him exactly what she was thinking.

"Get the bees situated?" Aunt Peavy asked when she returned.

"Yeah." Daisy yawned and stretched.

"That's good."

"Where's Travis?"

"Neela called and asked if Travis could come over for a fish fry. I thought it'd be okay to let him go on over, considering they are his grandparents."

"The Carmodys are home?"

Daisy hadn't seen Kael's parents since the day the alfalfa field burned. She'd talked to them over the phone before the wedding but that was it. She felt a little anxious, contemplating how their relationship had changed since Kael had told them about Travis.

Fear leaped into her chest. "They're not planning on telling Travis they're his grandparents, are they?"

"Oh, no. Neela and Chet understand that you and Kael want

to break the news to Travis in your own time."

"This is so strange having the Carmodys as my in-laws."

"Think how they feel," Aunt Peavy said. "Living next door for so long without knowing their only grandchild was just a few acres away."

Sighing, Daisy plunked down in a chair next to Aunt Peavy. "Rose certainly messed up everyone's life."

"Yes. Poor Rose."

"Poor Rose?" Daisy frowned. "Why does she get all the pity? She's the one who pretended to be me to seduce Kael and get pregnant with his child."

"Why?" Aunt Peavy gave Daisy a serious look. "Because Rose is dead."

"Like I don't know that? She was *my* twin sister." A wave of old resentment washed through her. It was unexpected and took her by surprise. "From the time Mom and Dad were killed, the only thing I ever heard was 'Poor Rose, she's barely holding up.' Or, 'You've got to forgive Rose, she isn't handling her parents' deaths very well.' What about me, Auntie? Didn't anybody ever think about me?"

Aunt Peavy looked contrite. "Sweetie, you were always so strong. There was no need to worry about you."

For the first time in ten years, she spoke her true feelings. "No need? I've become a bitter, unhappy woman, hiding myself away on this bee farm, devoting myself to my wayward sister's son. The child that she bore after sleeping with my boyfriend," Daisy said.

"Rose had a lot of problems, darlin'."

"Don't you think it affected me, too? I'm not a robot! I got tired of being the reliable one, of making all the decisions, of having to give up fun in favor of taking care of things. If someone had made Rose assume her share of the responsibility, if she'd been held accountable for her actions, I think she would be alive today."

Suddenly, the grief she'd been hanging on to since her parents' deaths burst from her in unstoppable torrents. "I miss her Auntie. I miss my twin sister so much!"

"Oh, love, you've been such a brave little thing." Aunt Peavy got up from her chair and went over to draw Daisy into her arms and cradle her against her bosom. "You're so right. I never had any children of my own; I didn't know how to raise two sixteen-year-old girls."

"I'm not blaming you," Daisy sobbed. "I'm blaming myself and Rose. I guess I'm even blaming Mom and Dad for dying. I know they couldn't control what happened, but I felt abandoned."

"Cry, sweetie, it's been a long time coming."

And she did, relinquishing her emotions to the choking sorrow that had dogged her for years.

They sat there for a time, Aunt Peavy gently rocking her back and forth, soothing Daisy as she often soothed Travis. "Everything's okay now. Kael's back."

*Kael's back.*

"You two have been gifted with a child and a chance to make everything right," Aunt Peavy continued. "Don't throw it away because you haven't forgiven your sister."

"What do you mean?"

"I see the way you've been treating Kael. Still punishing him for the mistake he made seven years ago. The man's aching for your approval, Daisy."

"Ha."

"Don't sound so skeptical. He's loved you for years."

"He hasn't told me that."

"Some men find those are tough words to say." Aunt Peavy pulled a tissue from her pocket and passed it to Daisy.

"And some men don't say those words because they don't mean them."

"Actions speak louder than words."

"That's right. And who ran off seven years ago?" Daisy asked.

"A boy ran away. A man came home. A man who's been trying to show you what he's become, but you seem blind to his efforts. Kael willingly assumed his responsibility once he knew Travis was his son. He married you, Daisy. Doesn't that tell you anything?"

"It still doesn't mean he loves *me*." Daisy blotted her face with the tissue. "And there's no proof he won't leave again when the going gets tough or when the lure of the road stirs his blood. I'm terrified he'll disappear on me again."

"There are no guarantees in life. I would have thought you'd have learned that lesson by now."

Daisy pondered her aunt's words. True enough, life was a precarious proposition. If only she could trust Kael. But the thought of abandoning control in favor of going with the flow terrified her.

"Feeling better?" Aunt Peavy inclined her head.

Daisy nodded. "I'm sorry I dumped on you like that."

"Posh." She waved a hand. "That's what aunts are for."

"You're the best," Daisy whispered, giving her a fierce hug.

"I think I better stay home tonight. You might need to talk some more."

"Stay home?"

"Don't you remember? I'm going to stay over at Jenny's."

"Oh, yeah. I forgot," Daisy said. "Please don't change your plans on my account. I'm fine."

"You sure?"

"Positive."

"If you're sure, then I better get my overnight bag packed." Aunt Peavy got to her feet.

At that moment, the landline rang.

"I'll answer it. You get ready." Daisy shooed Aunt Peavy toward the stairs, then picked up the phone.

"Hello."

"Daisy?"

"Mrs. Carmody." Daisy recognized the older woman's cool, dulcet tones.

"Please," she said. "You must call me Neela."

"Neela," Daisy amended.

"Now isn't that much nicer. Feels more like family."

"Yes," Daisy agreed, an unexpected warmness heating her heart.

"Listen, dear, Travis and Chet are having such a fabulous time playing video games, I was wondering if it would be all right if Travis spent the night."

Daisy hesitated.

"I know you and Kael haven't had a moment alone since you got married. Why don't you let Travis stay? We'll take him to church with us tomorrow, then bring him home. You can sleep in for once on a Sunday morning."

Travis had never been away from home overnight. She said as much to her mother-in-law.

"We're just next door. If he gets homesick, we'll bring him right home," Neela assured her.

"I don't know."

"Please, Daisy. We've got so much catching up to do with our grandson." Her voice hitched, and Daisy realized with a start the unflappable woman was fighting back tears.

"His pajamas," she said lamely, torn between wanting to share her son with his grandparents and needing to hold on to her authority. For six years, Travis had belonged to her exclusively. It was unsettling to realize she was forced to share him not only with Kael but with his parents as well.

"If you don't mind, I have some of Kael's old cowboy pj's Travis wants to wear."

"Sure," Daisy found herself saying.

"Thank you so much." Gratitude filled Neela's voice.

LORI WILDE

"You're welcome."

Daisy said goodbye, hung up the phone, and turned to see Aunt Peavy coming downstairs, her overnight bag tucked under her arm.

"Was that Jenny?"

"No. Neela. She wants Travis to spend the night."

"That's nice," Aunt Peavy said, a twinkle in her eye. "You and Kael will have the house all to yourselves."

Good thing he's in bed with bee stings, Daisy thought. Otherwise she might be in deep trouble. She'd done a lot of thinking today, and after talking to Aunt Peavy, she was weakening in her resolve not to consummate their marriage. Despite every effort she made to deny the attraction, Kael pushed all her buttons. It was increasingly difficult to be around him and not touch or kiss him.

"The effects of beestings only last a few hours, you know." Aunt Peavy winked as if reading her mind. "Kael should be right as rain once he sleeps off those antihistamines."

*Yes, and that's what I'm worried about*, Daisy thought.

A car horn tooted outside.

"That must be Jenny," Aunt Peavy said, hustling through the kitchen with surprising speed. "See you tomorrow, sweetie." She gave Daisy a little wave and disappeared out the door.

Instantly the house fell quiet. The grandfather clock in the hallway ticked loudly as if counting down the moments to some unknown destiny.

*Don't be melodramatic*, she chided herself, but Daisy couldn't shake the feeling that something monumental was about to happen. Inexplicably, she felt herself drawn toward the stairs.

Without consciously acknowledging it, Daisy moved in that direction. She straightened odds and ends about the room as she went. She plumped pillows that didn't need plumping, stacked books that were already even, brushed nonexistent lint from the furniture upholstery. Until at last, she stood breathlessly at the bottom of the stairs.

Taking the steps one at a time, she experienced a strange tightening in her chest. The floorboards creaked beneath her feet. Blood whooshed in her head. Her fingers tingled.

Inch by inch, she walked across the carpet. Finally, she rested her hand on the doorknob leading to Kael's room.

*Come on, Daisy, you're just checking to make sure Kael's okay. That's all. Don't read anything else into this.*

Squaring her shoulders, she eased open the bedroom door and slowly stuck her head inside.

Kael lay on his left side, his face to the wall. The covers had been kicked off and were trailing the floor. The ice pack she fashioned for his knee had ridden down his leg and now dangled from his ankle at an odd angle. A faint slash of waning sunlight seeped through the curtains and fell across his face, revealing that the swelling and redness were almost gone.

The door groaned as she pushed it wider, but Kael didn't move. Daisy stepped closer, her breath coming in quick and shallow gulps.

A strange sensation swept over her, as if she were standing outside her body, watching herself in action. She saw herself walk to the bed and oh, so carefully perch on the edge.

Kael mumbled something and hugged his pillow to his chest.

Daisy sat frozen to the sheets, her gaze transfixed on Kael's face.

A lock of hair drooped over his forehead, giving him a boyish appearance. His wide lips were slightly parted. His jaw was square, his nose straight and proud.

And his bare chest!

He must have taken off his shirt after she'd left him, for it lay in a tangle on the floor. His stomach was washboard flat.

There was no mistaking the body of a rodeo athlete. Firm. Strong. Muscled.

Heat swamped her body. She gulped past the desire blocking her throat.

What a man! So handsome. So masculine. So desirable.

And he was hers.

That was *her* gold band encircling his left ring finger. The mate to the one adorning her own finger. After years of hoping, praying, wishing, and dreaming, Kael was finally her husband, and she was entitled to the pleasures marriage could bring.

All she had to do was reach out and take him.

Daisy clutched her hands together to keep herself from touching him. No. She could not. She wasn't ready. Not in her mind, anyway.

Her body, however, was a different story. She ached for him deep down inside, hungry and savage, in a way she feared might never be sated.

Knees pressed together demurely, she leaned over to get a better look. A sheaf of her hair swung from her shoulder, grazing his cheek. Daisy held her breath. Was he awake?

He didn't flinch. Convinced he was still sleeping, she flipped her hair back over her shoulder and kept watching him.

She noticed a network of scars scattered over his body. Scars earned bull riding. Scars gathered like trophies.

There was a pale, puckered line on his right shoulder and another silvery slash under his neck, while yet a third jagged wound disappeared into the waistband of his jeans.

Tight, faded, unsnapped blue jeans.

Daisy gritted her teeth, bowled over by her lusty feelings.

On the one hand, those scars bugged her. He'd chosen to chase those scars, those ragged badges of honor, on the rodeo circuit instead of staying in Rascal with her. But on the other hand, she found his flaws alluring, and she was so proud of him.

To top it all off, the scars made her jealous.

He'd gotten those scars living an exciting life while she'd stayed home to shoulder the responsibilities that came her way.

She'd never been free to see the world, seek her fortune or discover who she truly could be.

But whose choice was that? No one had forced her to take over the farm after her parents died. Aunt Peavy and Rose had wanted to sell the honey farm. She, however, couldn't bear the idea. She'd been the one to convince them to stay.

Neither had anyone forced her to adopt Travis. She could have let him go into the foster system, but love wouldn't let her do it.

She had to stop blaming fate. Accept that she'd fully and freely chosen this life. Was proud of herself for her choices. Yes, choosing one path meant that she'd had to let go of other roads, but everyone had to do that. She wasn't special. She had no right to complain.

In that moment, she realized how she'd been punishing herself by not embracing the path she'd chosen. She'd only been looking at what she'd lost, not what she'd gained.

And right here, right now, she'd gained a husband.

*Husband.*

Kael was her husband.

Tentatively, she reached out a finger and lightly, delicately explored the one-inch scar just above his breast bone.

His skin quivered where she touched him, and Daisy panted against the furnace blast melting her insides.

*Kael.*

She'd loved him most of her life.

Was Aunt Peavy correct? Did Kael love her in return? If so, why didn't he say the words? Even when he was trying to convince her to marry him, he'd hadn't mentioned love. Well, except in that hastily scrawled note he'd posted on the fridge. That didn't count.

*But,* the tiny voice in the back of her mind argued. *Hasn't he shown you that he loves you?*

He helped with the bees and cleaned up around the house.

He brought her simple presents, a rose from the garden, her favorite candy bar from the grocery store, a full tank of gasoline in the truck.

Little things that added up to something pretty special. Things that spoke more than all the words in the world could say. He'd honored her wishes to sleep in separate beds. Most men would have pushed the issue. Kael had demonstrated that he was willing to work for this marriage.

Far more than she had.

Then today he'd shown himself to be a true hero. He'd sacrificed himself so Travis wouldn't get stung. Seven years ago, she wouldn't have thought him capable of it, but becoming a father had changed Kael. Changed him in ways that both thrilled and terrified Daisy.

*What if?*

She wanted her own children so badly. The idea brought a twinge of longing to her womb. From the time she was sixteen years old, she'd fantasized Kael as the father of her children. They would have her work ethic and his fearlessness. His easygoing ways and her determination. His hazel eyes and her auburn hair.

Now here he was, her husband. Lying almost naked in her bed.

What if they made love?

Her thoughts seesawed back and forth, pulling her first one way and then the other. Truth was, only time could tell whether these changes in Kael were real or not.

She continued to strum his skin lightly, savoring the delicious sensation, toying with dangerous notions, tempting fate.

Suddenly his hand snaked out, and he grabbed her wrist.

Shocked, Daisy's mouth flew open, and she stared into his wide-open eyes.

He was staring. Intently. His gaze lust-filled and hot.

For her.

## 🐾 11 🐾

"What do you think you're doing?" He growled under his breath.

Daisy tried to scramble off the bed, but he ensnared her waist with his other arm. "Let me go," she cried, pulling against him. Her voice was high and shrill.

"It's okay, Daisy, if you want to admire my body. But when you start touching me, you better be prepared to back up your invitation." He tugged her closer still, until she was pressed flat against him, chest to chest, their faces millimeters apart.

"Don't tease me." His expression was deadly serious. "I mean what I say. I can't stick to my promise to keep my hands to myself if you tease me."

"Please," she whispered, trembling with pent-up sexual tension.

"Please what?" he asked.

Her mouth opened, but no words came out. She was transfixed by the gaze in those hazel eyes.

"Do you want me to make love to you, Daisy?"

Yes! But, oh, how she wanted Kael to tell her that he loved

her, because, no matter how badly she might yearn for physical release, she needed to hear those words.

"How are the beestings?" she asked, quickly changing the subject as if the man beneath her wasn't a potent package of raw sexual energy just waiting to explode.

"The beestings are fine. They won't get in the way of love-making if that's what you mean."

"That wasn't what I meant!"

"Then why are you blushing?"

"Listen here, Kael, I didn't come in here to seduce you."

"No, you listen to me, Daisy. You crawled into *this* bed with me, stroked *my* bare chest. You started this—are you prepared to finish it?"

Daisy whimpered. "I don't know."

He stared at her a moment; their eyes locked, and her belly squeezed tight.

"That's a beginning," he whispered.

"I'm confused."

"I know." Tenderly, he traced a circle on her bare arm, and she shivered.

"Kael, I—"

"No need to explain. How's Travis? Did he get stung?"

"No, you saved him. He's spending the night with your folks."

"He is?" Kael mused, the gleam in his eyes glowing brighter. "Where's Aunt Peavy?"

"Sleeping over at her friend Jenny's house tonight."

"So, we're alone?"

Daisy nodded.

"Just you and me for the whole night?"

"Yes, but Kael, I can't, I don't." Daisy didn't even know how to explain the crazy-mixed-up feelings jumping around inside her.

"It's okay, sweetheart. I understand." He pushed her hair from her face, his callused fingers grazing her cheek.

"You do?"

"You need more time."

*No*, she thought, *I need you to tell me that you love me.*

"You need to be ready," he continued. "You're inquisitive, exploring, but I can see it in your eyes, you're still holding back. You're still wondering if I'll betray you again."

"Kael..."

"Shh." He placed his index finger over her lips. "Let me just hold you," he invited, nestling into the pillow.

Tears dusted her eyelashes, and she didn't even know why. She settled into the crook of Kael's arm and breathed in his heavenly scent. She could hear his heart thudding, so strong, so reassuring.

Kael curled himself around her, tucking his thighs against her bottom so that they spooned in the middle of that big bed.

It felt wonderful, having him here like this, exactly the way she'd imagined a thousand times over the years.

"You don't know how I've longed for this," Kael whispered as if reading her mind. His warm breath tickled the hairs on the back of her neck, causing Daisy to catch her breath. "Me and you, snuggling together as husband and wife."

*Husband and wife.*

The phrase, spoken in such a reverent tone, sent tiny shivers skipping down Daisy's spine.

Kael's grip tightened, and he tugged her closer. Every place their bare skin touched, Daisy's nerve endings sizzled and caught fire. She closed her eyes and drifted on the heavenly sensation, too weary to fight the attraction any longer. She loved Kael. He was her husband. Why shouldn't she savor this incredible feeling?

"Many a day, when I was on the road, only the dream of holding you in my arms again kept me going," he said, his voice

LORI WILDE

resonating in the room's small confines. "It was pretty darned lonely."

Daisy swallowed hard against the tide of emotions pushing her this way and that. "Then why didn't you come home?"

Kael was silent for a moment. "I guess I was trying to prove something."

"What were you trying to prove?" she asked, her stomach tensing as she waited for his answer. She'd never been able to understand why he'd chosen the rodeo circuit over a life with her. Perhaps now that they were older, Kael could explain things in a way that made sense to her.

"I suppose I was looking for my purpose in life."

"I never understood the appeal of risking your life on the back of a bucking bull."

"That's because you've always had a purpose, Daisy. First it was running the farm after your parents died and looking after Aunt Peavy and Rose. Then raising Travis." He sighed. "You assume the responsibility like a trouper. You knew what had to be done, and you did it."

"Go on," Daisy said.

"Me, I had nothing to show I was a man. I was raised in the lap of luxury; my parents are so wealthy I never needed to work. I'm an only child without any brothers or sisters to challenge me. I had everything on a silver platter, Daisy." He paused. "Except you."

"You could have had me, too."

"Not under your conditions, sweetheart. You wanted me to give up the one thing that gave me an identity."

"I didn't understand that," she said, squeezing his hand. "That was shortsighted of me."

"I wanted to marry you more than anything on earth, but I felt that I had nothing to offer until I'd made a name for myself. That's why I needed the rodeo, not because I didn't love you."

"You love me?" she whispered, her throat constricting against the warm rush rising inside her.

"Daisy, I've loved you all my life. Haven't you figured that out by now?"

She turned over in his arms, her eyes hungrily searching his face in the faint light barely seeping through the window. Fingers trembling, she reached out to touch his lips. "Is it true?"

"Nothing has ever been truer."

Daisy's heart thudded against her chest. She needed to believe him, more than she needed to breathe.

"Oh, Kael, why did you wait so long to tell me?"

"Because I knew I wasn't ready to get married. Not seven years ago. But I should have. I think we could have worked things out, come to an understanding and had a long engagement if it hadn't been for what happened between me and Rose."

Ah, there was that. The old familiar pang of betrayal rose in her.

Kael stared deeply into her eyes. "I'm so sorry for what I put you through."

"You really thought Rose was me?"

"Of course. I would never have cheated on you. Especially with your own twin sister. I'd waited for you for so long and when Rose came to me pretending to be you, it was the happiest night of life because I believed it *was* you." Kael's hazel eyes glistened with unshed tears. "I know there's a lot for you to forgive. I understand the anger you still carry, but Daisy, please, please, please know that I'd cut off my right arm if it would change things."

Daisy took a deep breath and laid her index finger against his lips. "Shh," she said. "No matter what happened, we can't really regret it. Otherwise we wouldn't have Travis."

"Sweetheart, you have no idea how much it cheers me to hear you say that."

"I did a lot of thinking today, Kael. You've made a huge effort these past few weeks to prove to me you'd be a good father. Today when you threw Travis in the pond and let the bees come after you, I knew you were serious."

"Dead serious, Daisy. I want us to be a real family and have a real marriage. Can you do that?"

As if the glacier inside Daisy's heart had collided head on with a flame thrower, the part of herself she'd frozen away for so long began, at last, to melt. She felt closer to Kael than ever before, not just physically, but emotionally as well.

Anger and betrayal vanished in the perfect cocoon of their love. Recrimination and reproach disappeared into the past. She had a choice to make. Forgive or hold on to her sorrow.

Daisy followed her heart. Tentatively, she scooted as close to Kael as possible, resting her lips on his.

His response was hungry and immediate. His mouth took hers with a gentle force. Tenderly, his tongue begged entry into her warm recesses, and Daisy let him in.

Throwing back her head, she moaned low and throaty. Threading her fingers through his hair, she pulled him down closer, deeper into the bed.

She wanted Kael. Here. Now. This minute. Without further ado. Arching her back, Daisy pressed herself into his body. She trembled with anticipation as a simmering heat, unlike anything she'd even known, warmed her in a soft, cozy glow.

"Kael, Kael, Kael," she chanted.

"My darling Daisy," he murmured, breaking their connection long enough to drop kisses onto her closed eyelids. "We've waited so long for this. I don't want to rush you. Are you sure you're ready?"

She answered by kissing him again, then looking straight into his eyes. "Make love to me, Kael. Consummate our marriage and claim me as your wife."

"At last." He sighed. "At long last." And the past dropped away as he held her in his arms.

※

KAEL WOKE WITH A SMILE ON HIS FACE. HIS ARM WAS NUMB FROM THE weight of Daisy's head resting on his shoulder, but he didn't care. He stared at her red hair spilling across the pillow like sun-burnished silk, and his heart filled with wonder.

Last night they'd made love for the first time. Soft, slow, and gentle. She'd opened up to him like a new flower reaching for the sun.

She was truly his wife now, in every sense of the word.

Somehow, he'd managed to sneak past the stone barriers she'd erected. Kael wasn't even sure how he'd convinced Daisy he was sincere. But it didn't matter how. All that counted was that they were together.

Only one more obstacle remained. Getting her to agree to tell Travis that he was the boy's father. Until they cleared that hurdle, they couldn't get down to the business of fully merging into a family.

Daisy's eyelashes fluttered open.

"Good morning," Kael greeted, his smile widening. He propped himself on one elbow and studied her. The cheerful glow streaming through the curtains accentuated the freckles that dusted the bridge of her nose and highlighted her determined chin.

Daisy reached for the sheet and tugged the covers high enough to hide her bare breasts. Grinning shyly, she said, "Good morning."

"How do you feel?" he asked.

She dropped her gaze but couldn't hide a knowing smile. "Pretty good."

"Pretty good?" He feigned mock indignation. "That's it?"

"Okay," she relented, pursing her lips slightly. "I feel marvelous. Last night was wonderful." She yawned and stretched her body, bowing her back with catlike grace.

Watching her sent hot desire racing through Kael's masculine engines. She'd better stop it, or he couldn't be held responsible for his actions.

"No regrets?" he asked, waiting warily for her answer.

Daisy hesitated, but for only a split second. That hesitation, however small, cleaved his heart. Did she have regrets?

"None," Daisy assured him.

"You sure?"

"I'm sure."

"'Cause if you're still worried about something, we need to talk it out." Kael caught his bottom lip between his teeth and waited expectantly.

Stubbornness, pride, and miscommunication had been at the root of their problems seven years ago, and he'd be danged if he'd allow miscommunication to separate them again. Not when they'd come this far. Not when they were so close to cementing the shaky foundation of the past.

She shook her head. "It's okay."

"Something's on your mind. I can see it in your face."

"I was just thinking about Travis."

"I woke up thinking about him, too," Kael said. "I'm ready to tell him that I'm his father."

"Wait a minute." Daisy secured the sheet under each armpit, then raised her palms. "You're moving too fast for me. We've got to think this through. No harm is going to come from waiting a while longer."

Kael took a deep breath. He supposed she was right, but darn it, he was ready to claim his son. "Okay," he conceded, "when?"

"I can't give you a definite time."

Exasperated, Kael ran a hand through his hair. "Why not?"

"Because," Daisy hedged, "I'm just not sure."

"You mean you still don't trust me." He bit the words off, and they fell brittle into the air. "Daisy, are you telling me last night meant nothing?"

"No."

"I thought we had made a start at repairing what we'd lost."

"We did make a start. But that's all it is, Kael, a start. There's seven years of heartache between us; it's not going to evaporate with one night of lovemaking."

"Not if you keep nursing a grudge like a sore tooth, it's not." He raised his voice, upset with her and upset with himself for having placed too many expectations on lovemaking.

"Lower your voice, please."

Kael clenched his jaw and forced himself to calm down. "All right. We'll do it your way. You let me know when you trust me enough to tell my son who I really am. I certainly hope it isn't on our fiftieth wedding anniversary."

❧

DAISY PEERED AT KAEL. HE LOOKED SUMPTUOUS PROPPED UP AGAINST the headboard, one arm

draped casually over his raised knee. His hair was mussed endearingly, and the bedcovers were tucked around his narrow waist.

If she reached out a few inches, she could brush his skin with her fingertips. That thought brought a lump of awareness into her throat. A vision of last night's passion flashed in her mind, and a heated flush crept up her neck.

She never knew she could surrender with such abandon. For years, she'd hidden her sexuality, secretly hoping against hope and waiting for the time when Kael came home. Their tender joining had been everything she had wanted and more—so much more. Now that she'd made love to him, the stakes intensified.

If he left her at this point, she'd be completely destroyed.

Daisy closed her eyes against the fear that sprang into her chest. Perhaps she'd been foolish to give herself to him last night. Heated passion mixed with years of pent-up emotions had overcome her. She'd surrendered to Kael. Actually, she'd been the one to initiate things.

But what was done was done, and she really couldn't regret the tenderness they'd shared.

What she could do, however, was protect Travis. She simply couldn't allow him to tell the boy the truth until she was one hundred percent certain Kael was home for good.

The upcoming rodeo next week was Kael's proving ground. They were supposed to attend a party at Joe Kelly's house. A party filled with Kael's adoring friends and fans, who would be encouraging him to have that experimental knee surgery and get back into the ring.

Could Kael resist? Could he really turn away from the rodeo? This time, could he choose love and family over bull riding? If he passed that test, then Daisy would let him tell Travis the news.

"Daisy?"

She glanced up to find Kael watching her with a serious expression on his face. Blinking, she met his stare and saw love for her brimming in his hazel eyes.

Her heart pounded. "Yes?"

He cupped her chin in his palm. "Don't you worry, sweetheart," he said, his voice thick with emotion. "I'm not going to let you down again. I swear it."

## 12

**D**espite Kael's reassurances, quelling her anxiety proved a monumental task as the rodeo drew closer. In the seven years Kael had been gone, she'd done her best to ignore the biggest annual event in Rascal.

But over the course of the past week, no matter how hard she threw herself into her work, she couldn't avoid the rodeo talk.

She went to the feed store to find Boss Martin and Kurt McNally shooting the breeze about the local boys competing in the bull riding event. While she got a trim at Dorothy's Curl-Up-and-Dye, the ladies quizzed her about Kael's injury. She drove down Main Street only to be confronted with red, white, and blue rodeo banners spanning the road.

It seemed as if a time bomb had been set in her brain, and Daisy was ticking off the minutes, just waiting for Kael's reaction. He'd promised her he had given up bull riding for good and that he wasn't going to have the surgery, but for Daisy, seeing was believing.

They'd planned on taking Travis to the rodeo, both agreeing that avoiding the event was not the answer.

Kael had to face his retirement and deal with the fallout. Daisy couldn't go on living not knowing if he'd gotten bull riding out of his system or if the old longing still lurked within. In her estimation it came down to one thing. Which did he care about most? Her and Travis or his career?

So, she waited with bated breath, fingers crossed and her heart on hold, for the man she loved to give himself to her completely with no holds barred and no regrets for what he was giving up.

❧

KAEL, TOO, FELT THE EFFECTS OF THE IMPENDING RODEO. THE excitement that skittered through the town plowed past him in a rush. It had been seven months since his misbegotten spill on the back of the Texas Tornado, seven months of physical therapy, a lot of pain, and a very major decision looming over his head.

Except, finding out that Travis was his son had altered everything. From his relationship with Daisy to his own self-image, Kael was not the same man he had been seven months earlier. Now he had a family to consider. He no longer had the luxury of making decisions based on his own wants and desires. For once, something meant more to Kael than fame, adulation, adventure, and proving himself.

The thing was, he embraced this wondrous new life with enthusiasm he'd never dreamed possible in the days of his youth.

Becoming a husband and father were the true tests of his manhood, not staying eight seconds on the back of some angry, snorting beast. To provide a solid, stable environment for his child, to offer his wife the love and affection she'd lost out on, to share with them both all the joy and happiness family life could bring—now that was a goal worth achieving.

Sure, Rascal's preoccupation with the rodeo sent a sweep of nostalgia through him, but that didn't mean he wanted to go backward in time. He'd been there. He'd participated. He'd been the star of the show, the golden boy. He'd had his glory in the sun. It was time to look forward.

To turn the reins over to the young guns who still had something to prove.

"Hurry up, you guys," Travis pleaded, hopping from foot to foot several yards in front of Kael and Daisy.

He was a miniature Kael, decked out in cowboy regalia, from his straw hat to his cowboy boots to his western-style shirt and sharply creased blue jeans. They'd all three made a special trip into Rascal the evening before just to get the outfit for Travis.

"All the good seats are gonna be taken by the time we get there," Travis complained.

They'd parked the pickup in the dirt lot behind the rodeo arena and followed the stream of people to the ticket gate.

"Hold your horse there, cowboy; give your mom and me a chance to catch up."

Travis rolled his eyes. "Slowpokes," he grumbled but smiled.

"He's changed a lot since you've been home," Daisy said, gazing at her child with a tender expression.

"He's opened up," Kael agreed. "He doesn't seem so shy since I've been taking him into town with me when I run errands."

"I kept him on the farm too much. I know that."

"You did the best you could," Kael soothed.

"You've been good for him."

"Thank you for saying so." Kael slipped his arm securely around her waist and kept most of his weight on his good leg so he wouldn't limp.

The past week had been tentative between them. He knew she was secretly waiting for him to dash off after the rodeo circuit again, but he wasn't about to break his promise to her.

Nothing matched the joy he'd found in becoming a father, and nothing had prepared him for the pride he felt for his son. He wouldn't jeopardize that feeling for the largest purse in the PBR.

They ambled through the entrance and around to the covered bleachers. Travis wriggled with excitement, his eyes growing as round as half-dollars as he took in the sights and sounds.

Cowboys perched on catwalks above the cattle pens. Cowgirls in showy costumes trotted by on horseback. Rodeo clowns performed antics for the gathering crowd. Everywhere they looked there were cowboy hats and boots and big belt buckles. Kael had broken out his lucky gold belt buckle for the occasion.

Several people shouted a greeting to Kael, and he raised his hand in response.

"Wow," Travis said, clearly impressed. "You sure know a lot of folks."

Kael rested his hand on his son's shoulder. "When you ride the circuit for seven years, you get to meet a lot of people."

"I'm going to be a bull rider when I grow up!" Travis declared.

A mix of emotions charged through Kael. On the one hand, he'd be proud to have his son carry on his career, but did he really want his child risking his life for the sake of a sport?

Shooting a glance at Daisy, he saw the boy's comment hadn't been lost on her, either.

"You can get any ideas like that right out of your head, young man. Bull riding is dangerous."

"Ah, Mom." Travis kicked at the dirt with the toe of his boot. "You never let me do anything fun."

Daisy opened her mouth but snapped it shut before she said anything. Kael leaned over to take her elbow and whisper in her ear. "Don't worry. He'll forget all about this. Last week, he wanted to be a fireman."

"Just don't encourage him," she whispered back. "Please."

KAEL

"Settle down, Mama Hen." He stroked her waist. "Come on, I see some good seats up ahead."

They clambered over the wooden bleachers, and Kael situated his family next to the bull chutes. "Okay," he said. "I'm taking orders. Who wants soft drinks?"

"I'll have a ginger ale," Daisy said.

"Root beer!" Travis said. "And cotton candy."

"Be right back."

Whistling to himself, Kael started toward the concession stands. It felt great to be back in the rodeo arena, if only as a spectator.

The robust smell of sawdust, leather, and cattle filled the air, teasing Kael's nostrils and coaxing his memory. If he weren't injured, if he wasn't with Daisy and Kael, he'd be on the catwalk right now, checking out the bulls and comparing notes with his *compadres.*

"Let it go, Carmody," he muttered. He got in the concession line but couldn't stop looking at the gates where cowboys milled, preparing themselves for the upcoming events.

A firm hand clamped down on his shoulder. "Will you look what the cat dragged up."

Kael turned to see his ex-manager, Randy Howard, grinning at him. Randy was a tall man in his late forties with a big belly and an even bigger smile.

"Hey, you old so-and-so." Kael clasped Randy's hand in a hearty handshake. "How you doin'?"

"Pretty good." Randy cocked back his head for a better look at Kael. "Marriage agrees with you."

Kael glanced at Daisy in the stands and smiled. "Marrying Daisy is the best thing I've ever done."

"Must be hard, though, footloose cowboy like yourself taking on a ready-made family. Tell the truth, you miss bull riding, don't you?" Randy swept his hand at the hustle and bustle around them.

"Well, it *is* more than family life that retired me," Kael said, touching his knee.

"That knee doesn't have to stop you," Randy said. "You know Tug Jennings came out of retirement last month after having that same surgery you need."

Kael hadn't expected the news to hit him so strongly. Three years ago, his chief competition, Tug Jennings, had suffered a knee injury. An injury identical to Kael's. To hear that Tug was competing again after the surgery left a strange hollowness in Kael's chest.

"Whenever you're ready to have the surgery, just say the word," Randy said. "I'd love to have you back as a client."

"That's not going to happen."

"No?"

"Nope."

"So, what are you doing to keep busy these days?"

"Beekeeping."

"Bee what?"

"I'm helping Daisy run her bee farm."

Randy hooted. "Never would have fingered a wanderer like you to turn bee farmer. Got to hand it to you, man. I could never settle for something so mundane."

"Beekeeping's not mundane," Kael said, feeling himself get defensive. He shouldn't let Randy goad him or let thoughts of Tug Jennings get the better of him. He'd made his choice, and he knew in his heart it was the right one.

"Well, listen, I gotta go. Got two cowboys ridin' this afternoon, but neither one is as good as you were."

*As good as you were.*

The words echoed in Kael's ears. Words people said to has-beens.

"Good luck with the beekeeping. Maybe you can send me a gallon of honey for Christmas." Chuckling, Randy headed off through the crowd.

Kael pulled the brim of his cowboy hat lower over his eyes and pushed aside Randy's derision. Think of Daisy, he told himself. And Travis. He knew they were worth the sacrifice. All Randy Howard had to show for his personal life was three ex-wives and two grown kids that wouldn't even speak to him.

Buying the refreshments, Kael headed back to the stands, the uneasy feeling heavy against his spine.

⚜

AFTER THE RODEO, LOADED WITH SOUVENIRS, THEY HEADED FOR JOE'S party. While Kael drove the few miles out of town, Travis chattered nonstop in the back seat of the truck. Daisy glanced at her husband. He'd been strangely quiet ever since returning from the concession stand.

"Is something wrong?" she asked him.

"Huh?" Kael jerked his head around to stare at her. "What?"

Daisy's lip trembled. It was just as she'd suspected. The lure of the rodeo had tightened its grip on him. Still, it wasn't an issue they could avoid. She had to know the truth. Could Kael really give it up?

"I saw the way you were watching those bull riders. You wanted to be out there, didn't you?"

"Please, Daisy, let's not get into this now." He sighed. "We're almost at Joe's."

She clamped her lips together in a tight line and folded her arms across her chest. Tears were dangerously close to slipping down her cheeks, but she'd be darned if she'd let Kael know exactly how upset she was.

He reached over to pat her knee, and she closed her eyes.

*I will not cry. I will not cry. I will not cry.*

Kael pulled into the driveway lined with vehicles and killed the engine. Immediately, guests poured from the house, Joe Kelly in the lead.

"What's going on?" Kael asked, climbing out of the truck.

"Surprise!" everyone shouted in unison.

"It's your retirement party, buddy." Joe jabbed him playfully on the arm. "We're glad to have you home for good."

Kael cast a glance back over his shoulder at Daisy who sat rigid in the front seat. "Hang on a minute." He raised his hand. Determined, he squared his shoulders and walked around to the passenger side of the pickup toward her.

Daisy watched him come, his brows drawn into a frown, his limp slowing him down not one whit. Her heart throbbed like crazy; he looked like a man on a mission.

He wrenched open the door. "Are you coming inside?"

His eyes met hers, and despite the pain welling up inside her, Daisy knew she wanted to be by his side more than any place on the face of the earth.

"My friends are throwing me a retirement party. As in 'you're never gonna ride again, Kael.' Understand? I'd be honored if you'd share this moment with me, Daisy."

He held out his hand, and she took it. How could she not?

Tamping back all her doubts and fears, she allowed him to lead her up the driveway, Travis scurrying along behind them.

Joe and the rest of the guests ushered them inside the rambling ranch-style home. Joe thanked Kael profusely for a freezer he'd bought for Kelly's Bar. That touched her, but then, Kael had always been generous with those he cared about.

Joe's wife, Pam, greeted Daisy, and she managed to smile and mumble a reply. Big parties made her nervous.

The smell of barbecue wafted on the breeze along with the squeals and laughter of children at play. The screen door slammed repeatedly as people flowed in and out of the house.

Overwhelmed by the buzz of activity, Daisy nestled into the curve of Kael's body. She wasn't accustomed to many people bunched together, and she suppressed the urge to run right back to the truck.

Everyone was all talking at once, whizzing a million questions at Kael. His face glowed as he fielded their inquiries concerning his knee, his retirement, and his plans for the future.

Daisy's heart dropped. *He loves this*, she thought. The attention, the admiration, the adulation. Even if he had exorcised the bull riding demons, how could a man like Kael ever be content with an ordinary life? She was foolish and selfish to expect it of him.

He was a people person, extroverted and self-confident in groups large or small. She was an introvert, shy and uncertain, unless she was dealing with folks one-on-one. They were so different. A myriad of contrasts lay between them. Black and white, day and night, bitter and sweet. Why in heaven's name had she ever thought this marriage would work?

But the one thing that gave her hope, the one gesture that had her reaching down inside herself to hold on to the tenuous happiness she'd found, was the fact that no matter where his attention lay, no matter who he was talking to, he kept his arm tucked firmly around her waist.

"Come on into the den." Joe ushered Kael, Daisy, and Travis into the crowded family room. "We've got a video montage of your rodeo career."

"What?" Kael looked both stunned and pleased, his gaze fixed on the big screen television mounted on the wall.

His image was splayed across the screen. Kael was decked out in his riding gear, chaps, gloves, hat, boots, and clinging to the back of a bucking Brahma, one hand flailing high in the air, the other gloved hand tucked under the rope.

Daisy sneaked a glance at her husband and saw he was mesmerized.

"Sit," Joe commanded, pushing Kael down onto a leather sofa, "and enjoy."

Swallowing hard, Daisy stepped back against the paneled wall and willed herself to fade into the background. Kael took

Travis on his knee and, leaning his head down, carefully explained everything unfolding on-screen to his son.

*I should never have married him*, Daisy thought. *It's like caging a wild bird.* Misery washed through her.

Thirty minutes passed. The show concluded, and thankfully Joe hadn't included the clip of Kael's last ride when he'd gotten stomped by the Texas Tornado. Daisy didn't think she could have tolerated seeing that play out.

Travis was beaming up at his father like he was a god sent straight from the heavens. People clapped Kael on the back, telling him that he was a credit to Rascal. Stunned, Daisy realized he didn't need her, had never needed her, and that had been the root of their problem all along. From the time she was a teenager, she had always been needed by someone. First by her parents to help run the farm, then by Rose and Aunt Peavy and later by Travis. The simple truth of the matter was that Kael had never needed anyone, and he wasn't likely to start now.

Daisy raised a hand to her forehead. She felt hot and breathless.

Joe offered Kael a beer, and Joe's wife came around with a platter of hors d'oeuvres. Kael got swallowed up in the crowd, and Daisy found herself pushed farther and farther away from him until she was standing in the kitchen.

"Mom?"

She looked down to see Travis standing in front of her. "Yes, son?"

"Can I go outside and see the baby calves with the other kids?"

Instinct told her to say no, to protect him as she always had, but Kael had taught her a valuable lesson. Travis needed to be around children his own age. She couldn't keep him tied to her apron strings forever.

"Go ahead, sweetie." She patted Travis on the back, then

watched him slip through the tangle of adults and out the back door.

"Here you are."

From her position in the corner of the kitchen where she'd retreated from the noisy throng, Daisy lifted her chin and met Kael's gaze. Love, clear and certain, swam in his eyes. He smiled, and she managed to return it.

"I wondered where you'd gotten off to."

"Don't worry about me," she said. "Go on and have fun with your friends."

"Daisy, nothing is any fun without you by my side." His tone was serious.

"Do you mean that, Kael? Truly?"

"May I be struck dead if I'm lying."

She sucked in her breath, unable to wrench her gaze from his.

Kael held out his arm. "Come on."

She placed her hand in his and allowed him to lead her into the den where Joe was calling for a toast.

"Here's to the guest of honor," Joe said, perching himself on the hearth and raising his glass. "One heck of a bull rider. Good luck in your new life, Kael!"

There was a hearty round of cheers and the clinking of glasses. "Speech!" someone hollered.

"Yeah," someone else chimed in.

There were whistles and catcalls egging him on.

It didn't take much to convince him. Glowing with good-natured sheepishness, Kael took Joe's place by the mantel and thanked everyone for the wonderful party.

Standing there, watching her husband and his adoring fans, sent a jolt of pride flashing through her. It was easy to love Kael, with his good looks and his agreeable ways. He could have his pick of the women assembled in this room. And yet he'd chosen her. Why? She wasn't the easiest person to get along with.

Every doubt and fear she'd ever had about their relationship bubbled to the surface.

"And I just want you folks to know, that although a chapter is closing in my life, a whole new book is waiting to be written with my wife, Daisy, and my son, Travis."

Kael looked over at her, love shining brightly in his eyes.

But Daisy couldn't bear to gaze upon him. He might believe he wanted to settle down, but she knew better. Kael should have that knee surgery and go back to bull riding. It was what he loved most. It defined him. Without that wild spirit, who was he? Hadn't that footloose wildness always been the thing that attracted her to him, even as it kept them apart?

Through Kael she lived vicariously, enjoying the adventures and the adulation secondhand without having to put herself at risk. He'd been right to leave her seven years ago. There was no way the tortoise and the hare could successfully make a go of it.

Ducking her head, she turned away.

From outside the raised window, a sudden scream rent the air.

"It's one of the kids!" Pam Kelly said.

In seconds, a half-dozen adults pulled open the back door and tumbled into the yard, Daisy and Kael right behind them.

"What's going on?" she asked, fear pulsing through her.

Kael gripped her hand. "Where's Travis?"

"Criminey," a man said, pointing, "the kids are in the bull pen!"

A gaggle of children ran to the house, screaming and hollering. Joe's wife grabbed her daughter. "What's the matter? What happened?"

"That little red-haired boy—" the girl gasped, clutching her chest. "He tried to ride Ferdinand. He said he was gonna be a bull rider like his daddy."

Daisy's heart stopped. A ringing sound started in her ears

and rose to a terrifying crescendo. No. It couldn't be true. Not her boy. Travis, her shy, quiet child trying to ride a bull?

Kael dropped her hand and took off running. Daisy tried to follow, but her legs refused to move. She stood helpless, eyes fixed on Kael as he ran to the bull pen.

Minutes later he returned to the house, Travis cradled against his chest, a ring of spectators trailing after him. He was limping heavily, and tears slid helplessly down his cheeks.

Pam Kelly draped an arm around Daisy's shoulder, but she felt too numb to notice.

"Daisy..." Kael croaked, anguish on his face.

Travis rested in his arm, rag-doll limp. His face was the color of chalk, and his head lolled in the crook of Kael's elbow.

She seemed to float above her body, detached from what was going on around her. People were speaking in hushed whispers, gathering their own children to them.

"He climbed on the bull." Kael's voice trembled. "He was pretending he was me. Ferdinand shook him off like a flea. He hit his head. There's a big knot. He's unconscious."

Kael's shoulders shook violently as he sank to his knees, Travis still clutched tightly in his arms.

"Oh, God," Kael cried. "I caused this. I'm responsible."

"I called an ambulance," Joe said.

"Here's his hat, ma'am." Joe's son, Scott, a tow-haired boy only a few years older than Travis, extended the straw cowboy hat to Daisy.

Numbly, she took the hat and fingered the scratchy straw, then mumbled, "Thank you."

Scott nodded solemnly and stepped aside.

"Daddy loves you, Travis," Kael whispered into the boy's hair. He was alone on his own island of grief. "I'm sorry, so sorry."

Calmly, Daisy sank to her knees beside Kael. She reached out and traced her fingers over Travis' face. "Honey," she whispered, "it's Mama. Wake up now."

She willed him to open his eyes, to wrap those slender little arms around her and giggle, but he did not stir.

"If only I hadn't taken him to the rodeo. If only I hadn't let him watch those videos. If only I hadn't told him he could be a bull rider someday." Kael moaned.

"Travis," Daisy said. "Stop teasing us. You've got to open your eyes."

"Daisy." Kael met her stare at last, the regret on his face too much to bear. "Travis is unconscious."

"No," she denied. "He's not. He's only fooling around." She took the boy's arm and shook it. "Travis, stop this right now, you hear me?"

"Don't, Daisy, please," Kael begged.

God, no. Not a coma. He's just a little boy. Old memories rose up to slap Daisy. She remembered the state trooper standing on the front porch, his hat in his hands, his head bowed as he gave her and Rose the news that their parents had been killed in an automobile accident on the Interstate between Rascal and San Antonio transporting honey to a candy factory. She recalled the frantic phone call from New Orleans that had come in the middle of the night. It was Rose's boyfriend of the week. The man said he'd come home to find her unresponsive on the bedroom floor, an empty pill bottle and whiskey beside her.

Daisy clenched her hands, her nails biting into her palms. Not again. She couldn't bear to lose another loved one. Not Travis. Not this young. Not this way.

"Daisy, say something."

"Kael," she cried, agony rushing through her like a flooded river fleeing its banks. "What have you done to our son?"

The stark white hospital corridor stretched endlessly between the waiting room and the emergency department, where the paramedics had taken Travis. Overhead the fluorescent lights hummed and flickered.

Patients and their families sat like flour sacks on the cheap plastic benches, sighing, groaning, and waiting their turn with long-suffering acceptance. Occasionally, the intercom crackled. A staticky voice paged some hospital personnel to one area or the other. Housekeeping ordered to clean a spill in the cafeteria. Respiratory therapy needed to give a treatment in ICU.

The nursing supervisor should pick up an outside call on line two.

Kael noted all these things in a dull, detached manner. A sharp, antiseptic stench permeated the air, goaded his brain and caused him to recall that night, not so long ago, he'd been wheeled into a similar hospital, bleeding and alone.

Absentmindedly, he reached down and rubbed his aching knee. He knew what Travis was going through in there, and he almost choked on the empathy.

His son was hurt, and it was all his fault.

Kael bowed his head and sank his face in his hands. He'd encouraged Travis' interest in bull riding. Secretly, he'd been thrilled to see the influence of his genes surfacing in the boy. Egged on by macho egotism, he'd puffed up over the changes in his child. Under his sway, Travis had gone from hesitant and introverted like Daisy to enthusiastic and adventuresome like himself.

Only, those changes brought trouble.

Trouble he'd never anticipated.

Having a kid was scarier than he'd ever realized. When he'd discovered he had a son, his thoughts centered on all the fun they would have together. He'd never considered the flip side.

Just as he had with everything else in life, Kael had leaped in with both feet, never looking to see how secure the ground was beneath him.

Daisy was right. He *was* irresponsible, and that irresponsibility might cost his son his life.

A violent shudder ran through him. He should have stayed away from Rascal. Daisy and Travis had done fine without him. Now he had ruined everybody's life by coercing Daisy into marrying him.

*Daisy.*

At the thought of his wife, deep emotions prodded his chest. It hurt his heart to know what he'd done to her.

Right now, she was in with Travis. The doctor had said one parent in the room at a time. Kael insisted she go first.

Joe Kelly and the rest of the well-wishers had departed from the hospital long ago, murmuring words of sympathy and expressions of concern. Kael's parents brought them an extra vehicle, so Daisy wouldn't get stranded if Kael needed to go check on the farm or get food. His folks stayed for hours until Kael urged them to go home and get some rest.

He watched them go with a mix of relief and despair. He was

glad not to have to keep up a brave front, but on the other hand, he didn't relish the idea of being alone.

"Mr. Carmody?"

Kael looked up.

A young nurse in her early twenties stood before him, a red stethoscope around her neck, a back support belt encircling her waist, and a clipboard tucked in her arm.

Kael got to his feet and caught his breath. He searched the nurse's face for some indication of the news. Her eyes were guarded, her expression somber. Fear squeezed his gut. "Yes?"

She awarded him a faint smile, and he relaxed instantly, warm relief swimming through him.

"Your son just woke up. He seems to be fine, but to be on the safe side, the doctor wants to hold him overnight for observation. We'll take him up to a room in a few minutes, and you can see him there."

Kael let out his breath in a rush, his legs wobbly beneath him. "Thank you," he said, gratefully shaking her hand. "Thank you for everything."

"You're welcome," she smiled again, then disappeared back through the swinging double doors from where she'd emerged.

He hesitated a moment, swaying like a tree in the wind. Should he stay? Should he go? What would be best for Travis and Daisy?

He loved them both with such a fierce, abiding love. More than anything in the world, he wanted to be with them. The lure of the rodeo could never compare with what he'd found waiting for him here at home in Rascal.

And yet, he loved them so much he knew he must act in their best interest and not his own. Nothing mattered but Travis and Daisy and their well-being. Not his career, not what his parents thought of him, not even what he wanted out of life. He was a husband and a father. His family came first. Now and forever.

And they would be better off without him.

Kael supposed he'd arrived at the decision hours ago, sitting here alone in this godforsaken waiting room. He was a bad influence on his son. He'd led him into danger. There was no excuse for his actions. None. He couldn't ask Daisy's forgiveness. He didn't deserve it.

He'd leave town tomorrow after transferring money into Daisy's bank account. Then he'd go see his lawyer about drawing up divorce papers so Daisy could have her freedom. After that, he would call Randy Howard and tell him he was prepared to go through with the experimental surgery. What did it matter if he ended up crippled? Without Daisy, life wasn't worth enjoying. And if the surgery was a success, he could at least bury his sorrow in the only solace he had left—bull riding.

Pivoting on his heels, he spun toward the pneumatic doors. They opened before him, depositing him into the starless night. He was glad now that Daisy hadn't allowed him to tell Travis that he was the boy's biological father. His leaving would be less traumatic this way. Daisy had been wiser than he. Or she knew him better than he knew himself.

His spirits dragging lower than a snake's belly, Kael hitched in his breath and headed for his pickup, his heart dropping faster with each retreating step. Leaving the extra vehicle his parents had brought for Daisy.

Don't look back, he told himself. She doesn't need a sorry sack of cow dung like you messing up her life.

He got in the truck and started the engine, tears blinding his vision. He brushed them away with the back of his hand.

"It's for the best, Carmody," he said. "Everybody knows you're too danged irresponsible to be a good dad."

"HAVE YOU SEEN MY HUSBAND?" DAISY ASKED THE NURSE WHOSE picture ID proclaimed her "Susan Karns."

Susan shook her head. "Not since I told him we were taking Travis to the floor, Mrs. Carmody. That was..." She glanced at her watch. "...over forty minutes ago."

*Mrs. Carmody.* She liked the way that sounded. "Would you mind checking the waiting room for me?" she asked. "I know he'd like to go upstairs with us."

"Sure." Susan nodded. "Be right back." She turned and disappeared out the door.

"How you feelin', cowboy?" Daisy said, going over to the gurney and curling her fingers around the bedrail. She smiled down at her son.

"My head kinda hurts." Travis raised his head and tenderly fingered his scalp.

"You're going to stay off the back of bulls from now on, aren't you?" she chided, drawing the covers up more tightly around his neck and kissing his cheek.

"It's harder than it looks," Travis said. "I guess that's why Dad told me I couldn't ride a bull until I was twelve and that was only with his supervision."

"Kael told you that?" Daisy was surprised.

"Uh-huh."

"Why did you disobey him?" she asked sternly.

"The other kids dared me."

Daisy clicked her tongue. "Travis, you know better than that."

"Yeah," he gave her a snaggletoothed grin, and she was so happy to have him awake and healthy that she wrapped him in a bear hug.

There was a light rap on the door, and Susan stuck her head in. "Your husband wasn't in the waiting room. Maybe he went to the cafeteria for a cup of coffee?"

"Maybe. Thanks for checking."

"You're welcome. Let me just sign off Travis' chart, and I'll be right back to escort you to the floor."

Daisy bit down on her bottom lip. Where had Kael gone? She

needed to talk to him and let him know she'd been doing a lot of soul searching. These tense past hours spent alone in the emergency room, holding Travis' little hand while he lay unconscious on the stretcher had struck her with harsh reality.

If she continued her stubborn behavior, she would lose Kael forever. He'd been so good to take whatever she dished out, patiently deflecting her anger. She'd been punishing him for too many years.

Whatever had happened between him and Rose had been over a long time ago. He'd made his amends. And even though Travis had gotten injured trying to be a bull rider, could she ultimately hold Kael accountable? Didn't the positive changes he'd wrought in her son's life outweigh the negative? She couldn't deny that under Kael's influence Travis had blossomed.

And what about herself? Kael had worked his magic on her as well, peeling back all the old hurt and pain and replacing it with love.

Kids got hurt every day. If anyone were to blame, it was her. She should have been supervising Travis more closely.

She had to admit that just knowing Kael was out there waiting for them, that she wasn't going through this experience alone, gave wings to Daisy's heart. It was nice to have someone to lean on. A husband who cared.

Swallowing past her guilt, Daisy blinked. Kael had made mistakes, yes, but so had she. For the sake of their son, for their marriage, it was time she released all resentment. She forgave Rose, and she forgave Kael, but most of all Daisy forgave herself. For it was she who had most suffered the effects of her own hardheaded pride.

Daisy glanced at her watch and was surprised to discover it was only eleven thirty. It felt as if eons had passed since Travis' accident instead of four hours. So much had happened in such a short period. Her attitude had shifted one-hundred-eighty degrees. She gulped and pushed against her eyelids with her palms.

This time Kael was standing by her. He was her husband, her friend, and now her lover, and more than anything she wanted to wrap her arms around him and tell him so. Oh, how she loved that man! Had loved him since she was sixteen years old.

She shouldn't have taken her fear out on Kael by treating him with such cold disdain, especially in front of his friends. He loved Travis as much as she did. He was worried and probably heaping a pile of guilt upon his own head. When she should have been comforting her husband, she'd fallen back into her old behavior and had lashed out at him, blaming him for something that wasn't his fault.

It had been easy to accuse Kael. He accepted her acrimony as his due. Following old patterns, she'd taken the path of least resistance when she should have been looking to him for comfort. That's the way committed couples handled things. Together, as a team, not walling themselves off in their separate misery. Love could heal. Reproach would not.

It was hard for her. For years she'd had no one to depend on. She'd been strong for so long that she didn't know how to rely on anyone. Even when sheltering arms had been extended to her with no demands made, no strings attached, she'd been unable to accept Kael's unconditional love.

To embrace his love meant she'd have to relinquish her arrogant pride, and until this moment she'd been unwilling to loosen her grip on the one thing that had kept her going through life's tragedies.

Where was Kael? She had so much to say to him, to let him know the time had come to tell Travis he was his father.

"Ready?" Susan Karns popped through the door, Travis' chart in her hand, a cheerful smile on her lips.

Daisy nodded. "If you do happen to see my husband down here, please send him up to our room."

"Will do. Ready for a ride, young man?" Susan grinned at Travis.

"Not on a bull!" he exclaimed.

"Good answer," Susan replied, kicking off the brake on the stretcher and wheeling it through the door.

A few minutes later, after they'd settled into the room and Travis had drifted off to sleep, Daisy texted Kael but didn't get an answer. She texted him again. Waited.

She sat in a rocking chair next to Travis' bed in the pediatric ward, the night-light against the floorboard the only illumination in the room. Nervously, she consulted her watch. Ten minutes passed. Then fifteen, then twenty. Why wasn't he answering her texts?

Maybe he was tired. Maybe he went home to rest.

Then Daisy shook her head in the darkness. Without letting her know? Without seeing Travis first? She could understand if Kael was upset with her and didn't wish to speak to her right now, but she couldn't imagine him leaving without saying good-night to his son.

The rocking chair creaked when she got to her feet. Picking up her cell phone, she carried it into the bathroom and shut the door so she wouldn't disturb Travis.

Her stomach felt queasy. Pressing a hand to her abdomen to stifle the butterflies, she punched in the number of her landline at home.

Aunt Peavy answered on the seventh ring. "Hello?" she mumbled. Clearly, she'd been asleep.

"Auntie, it's me, Daisy."

"Where are you, sweetie?"

"I'm at the hospital. Did you hear about Travis?"

"Yes, Kael told me. How is he?"

"Doing well. He's asleep right now. They took X-rays and did an MRI. Nothing showed up. The doctor wants to keep him overnight to be on the safe side. We'll be home in the morning."

"That's good." Her aunt's voice sounded concerned, guarded.

Odd chills raced up Daisy's spine. "Auntie, by any chance is Kael there?"

Aunt Peavy hesitated.

"What's wrong?" Daisy asked.

"Sweetie, I'm afraid I've got some bad news."

Daisy sank down on the closed toilet lid, her heart fluttering in despair. Had something happened to Kael?

"What is it?" she whispered, bracing herself for bad news.

"Kael left."

"Excuse me?"

"Kael came home, told me what happened, said Travis' accident was all his fault, and you'd both be better off without him."

Pushing her fingers through her hair, she sat trying to make sense of Aunt Peavy's words. "What do you mean?"

"He packed his clothes, cleared out his things. He's gone, Daisy. Says he's going to give you a divorce, have that knee surgery, and go back to bull riding."

Stunned, Daisy hung up the receiver without even saying goodbye. The place where her heart had once resided was now a gaping chasm. She felt as if she were tumbling into a black hole of endless isolation.

Then the strong, hard-edged voice that had gotten her through so many woes resonated firm and clear in her head. *Well, fine. If he wanted to leave, then okay.*

She'd known all along it was foolish to place stock in Kael's longevity as a husband.

*It's gonna be okay,* she coached herself. *You and Travis got along without him for seven years. You can get along without him for seventy. Who needs the likes of Kael Carmody, anyway?*

Her, that was who.

A sorrow more profound than anything she'd experienced since her twin sister's death wrapped an icy grip around Daisy's midsection. She tried to shrug it off, to deny the pain worming its way deep inside her, piling on top of all that other pain and hardening into something solid and ugly, but she couldn't.

Just when she'd been stupid enough to believe Kael had changed, that they had a good chance of building a real life together, he abandoned her again.

Tears overtook her.

Daisy sank down onto the floor and curled into a ball, her head resting on the cool tile. She felt sick. Sick and weak and so lonely.

"Kael," she whimpered. "Why, why?"

## ❧ 14 ❧

**K**ael drove straight through the night. Dawn's pink fingers streaked the sky by the time he reached Oklahoma City. Randy Howard had given him the name of Tug Jennings' knee specialist in Kansas City, and Kael had taken off with that destination in mind and no other plans.

For the past seventeen hours, he'd done nothing but drive and think of Daisy. Beautiful, hardworking, obstinate Daisy.

His wife.

He didn't deserve her. He never had. That's why it was best to forget her. Let her get on with her life and stay out of her way.

Except he couldn't get her off his mind. She was so tough, so strong, so passionate. Just when he thought he might never make headway with her, she'd let down her guard and started to trust him. Trusted him enough to let him make love to her.

*Ah, Daisy.*

The pain that shot through Kael's gut almost brought tears to his eyes. He'd betrayed that tentative trust.

He pulled into the parking lot of a donut shop, intending to get out and fetch himself some breakfast. Instead, he remained welded to the seat. He stared unseeingly through the plate-glass window at the waitress pouring coffee for two policemen perched on bar stools. The yeasty scent of donuts permeated the surrounding air, but it did not entice his appetite. He felt as if he might never eat again.

Taking a deep breath, Kael leaned his forehead against the steering wheel and stared down at his left leg. Covered in blue jeans, it looked normal. Gingerly, he fingered his kneecap.

Did he really want to go through surgery, rehab, and recovery just so he could climb on bulls and risk hurting himself even more severely the next time around? Was he brave enough to take the gamble, knowing as he went into the deal that the miracle surgery could backfire, leaving him with a permanent limp? What would it prove if he did win another PBR event?

Kael snorted. Bull riding had always been about proving himself. He'd thought if he could tame one of those wild critters, it meant he could conquer anything. He was wrong. Dead wrong. Bull riding proved nothing except that he was dumb enough to climb on the back of a wild animal and hang on tight.

Now that he had arrived at this place in his life, the whole business seemed mighty stupid. Truth being, he didn't really want to have the surgery. What he wanted was to be back with Daisy and Travis.

But he didn't belong there. He had no business being a husband and father. He'd put himself to the test and failed miserably. Because of his irresponsible influence, Travis had been hurt, and he'd caused Daisy needless suffering.

Daisy was right. He wasn't a real man at all, simply an irresponsible guy playing rodeo cowboy.

Kael raised his head and stared at himself in the rearview mirror. What he saw reflected there was not a pretty sight.

"This is your life, Kael. What's it gonna be? You gonna keep running and hiding from the best thing that ever happened to you or embrace it?"

Hazel eyes stared back at him. Eyes that looked exactly like his son's. In that instant, he knew what he had to do. There was only one answer.

Taking a deep breath, Kael keyed the engine and headed for his destiny.

☙❧

"LOOK, MAMA," TRAVIS CALLED OUT, POINTING A FINGER TOWARD THE road. "Car's coming."

Daisy looked up. She and Travis were in the field next to the Carmody Ranch, licking honey from their fingers. She'd been tending the hives, taking comfort in the one thing that remained constant in her life no matter what happened.

Bees.

Steady, hardworking creatures that they were, the new colonies were doing well. Although it was too late in the year to harvest honey, next year's crop promised to be a good one. Thanks to Kael's intervention and the money he'd left her.

Travis had joined her just as she was completing her work for the day and asked for a honeycomb to chew on. Daisy had extracted a chunk of the sweet, waxy treat and indulged herself as well. The succulent taste of raw honey invaded her mouth as she chewed.

The doctor had released Travis from the hospital the day before, and it seemed he'd suffered no ill effects in his tumble from Ferdinand's back. The boy had asked about Kael a dozen times, and Daisy hadn't yet had the heart to tell him he wasn't coming back.

Instead, she'd said Kael had gone away to have knee surgery. That much was true enough. What she'd tell her son in a week or two or ten, she didn't know. In actuality, Daisy herself hadn't recovered from the shock of Kael's leave-taking. Even though she thought she'd braced for it, she'd really begun to believe that he had changed.

"Looks like a pickup," Travis commented, scrambling up on the wooden split-rail fence for a better vantage point.

"Be careful," Daisy cautioned, reaching out a hand to stabilize him. "Don't fall."

"Mom," Travis chided with a long-suffering sigh. "I'm okay."

It took supreme effort, but she backed away and left him alone. If nothing else, this painful episode with Kael had shown her she needed to loosen the apron strings where Travis was concerned.

"It's Dad!" Travis exclaimed, his eyes lighting like beacons.

"It can't be." Daisy shook her head.

"It is! It is!"

"Sweetie, Kael's in Kansas City having knee surgery."

"No, he's not," Travis interrupted. "He's in our driveway." Lickety-split, Travis climbed down from the fence and tore out across the pasture, running at full throttle.

Daisy stood rooted to the ground. *It can't be.*

But it was.

The truck door slammed, and Kael got out. He walked straight toward Travis, caught the boy in his arms, and swung him high into the air. Sheer delight crossed the faces of both father and son.

Curiously, Daisy's pulse slowed, and the blood whooshed loudly in her ears. Kael lifted Travis over his head and settled him on his shoulders. Travis' happy giggles filled the air and sent hope soaring in Daisy's heart. She twisted her fingers in a knot and waited.

The wind blew the scent of sun, hay, and honey across the field. Her gaze rested on Kael's face. His jaw was determined, his chin set, but his eyes were kind, friendly, and encouraging.

"Daisy," he murmured.

"Kael."

They stared at each other, both wanting to embrace, but each afraid to make the first move.

Kael took Travis from his shoulders and set him on the ground. Then Kael squatted beside him. "I've got something to tell you," he said.

"You won't be having an operation?" Travis asked.

"That's right." Kael slanted Daisy a look. "I decided I don't want to be a bull rider anymore. It's no fun getting hurt."

"That's true!" Travis' eyes widened, and he fingered his scalp. "My head still hurts where I fell off Ferdinand."

"Next time I hope you think before you do something foolish like that," Kael chided.

"Yes, sir." Travis nodded.

"Good boy. Now listen to me a minute."

Daisy lifted a hand to her throat, uncertain what he was about to say.

Kael cleared his throat. "I'm your real father, Travis."

"I know." Travis beamed.

"How do you know?" Kael frowned and looked at Daisy. "Did you tell him?

Daisy shook her head.

"I just know." Travis shrugged.

Kael rocked back on his heels. "I'm sorry I wasn't here for you when you were little. Truth is, I didn't know you were my son until I came back to Rascal and your mother told me."

"It's okay." Travis gifted him with a smile. "You're home for good now."

"You are home, aren't you?" Daisy asked.

Kael stood up. "Yes, Daisy. I'm home for good."

"Travis," she said. "Why don't you go wash up for supper. Your father and I will be there in a minute."

"Do I have to?" Travis whined.

"You heard your mother," Kael said, never taking his eyes from Daisy's face. "Go wash up."

Like a shot, the boy headed for the house.

"Why did you leave?" She asked, once Travis was out of hearing range. "Why did you put me through that again?"

Tears misted his eyes. "I'm so sorry. I never meant to hurt you a second time. I just figured you and Travis were better off without me."

"Whatever gave you that silly idea, Kael?"

"If I hadn't been here, Travis would never have been brave enough to crawl up on that bull by himself. Me being a showoff is what spurred him to do that."

"Bit egotistical, aren't you?"

"It's true. Because of me your quiet son became an unruly youngster."

"Under your influence, Kael, *our* son has come out of his shell. He talks. He laughs. He makes friends. He's happy now where he wasn't before."

"What are you saying, Daisy?"

"I'm saying you're good for him, or hadn't you noticed?"

❧

A WARM, TINGLING SENSATION STARTED IN KAEL'S BELLY AND WORKED its way throughout his whole body. Was he hearing her correctly? Was she forgiving him?

Kael doffed his cowboy hat, hooked it over the fence post, and ran his fingers through his hair. He had so much to tell her, so much to be forgiven for. "You were right all along. I behaved irresponsibly. Because of me, our son was injured. Daisy, it could have been severe."

"But it wasn't."

"He could have been maimed for life like his old man." Kael ruefully swept a hand at his own knee.

"So, your answer to a tough problem was to pack up and run away?" She crossed her arms over her chest, staring at him in the way that a prosecuting attorney might stare down a perjuring witness.

"That was my initial response," Kael admitted. "I got scared. Terrified that if I stayed, I would unwittingly hurt you and Travis in a million other ways. But I made it as far as Oklahoma City before I realized I just couldn't do it. I love you and Travis with all my heart and soul."

"Do you love us enough to stick out the rough times as well as the good? Are you in for the long haul, Kael, when things are just flat boring? Can you give up bull riding and settle down once and for all?"

He stepped the few feet between them and caught her hands in his. He met her gaze and held it tight. "Yes, Daisy, I can. Over the course of the past few weeks, getting to know my son, falling in love with you all over again, I've learned there's no bigger thrill, no greater challenge than being married and raising a child."

It killed him to think she might not take him back, but she would be well within her rights.

"I love you, Daisy," he said and doffed his Stetson. "Will you take me back?"

༺✿༻

"WHY SHOULD I TRUST YOU?" SHE PULLED AWAY FROM HIM AND SAW the hurt on his face.

How she wanted to believe him! To know she could count on him now and forever. To know he'd be waiting for her no matter what happened. To wake up every morning in those strong arms and to go to sleep each night, wrapped in the glow of their love. The love that had remained unbroken despite mistakes, misunderstandings, and seven years' separation.

"I bought the ranch from my dad," Kael said. "I'm taking over the business. I canceled my knee surgery. And I got this for you."

He reached into his pocket and pulled out a small black box and passed it to her. With trembling fingers, Daisy took the gift. Tentatively, she opened it, and her breath caught in her chest.

A gorgeous one-carat diamond solitaire that eclipsed the gold band he'd bought her before, winked in the sunlight.

Kael took her hand and slipped the ring on her finger. "Will you marry me again, Daisy Hightower? This time for real. Not because you need money or because Travis needs a father but because I love you and I want to commit to you. In good times and bad, in sickness and in health,

for the rest of my natural life." His hazel eyes pleaded, and Daisy, washed away in the vortex of emotions, simply nodded.

Kael pulled her into his arms and kissed her—sweetly, tenderly, hopefully.

"From now on, we talk things out. No more running away from me and no more hiding behind your pride. Agreed?"

"Okay." She smiled at him, and a joy unlike anything she'd ever known rushed through her. At last. At long last, he was truly her husband.

"I've loved you since that time I first kissed you in the honey house," he said. "Remember?"

"How could I forget?" Daisy blushed at the memory. She'd just shown him how to steal the comb without upsetting the bees. The honey house had been hot, his kiss even hotter.

"You taste the same now as you did then—sweet, delicious, and tempting." He gazed at her with desire in his eyes and brushed a strand of hair from her face. "Know what I'm think-ing?" he asked, inclining his head toward the honey house.

Daisy giggled, and the sound filled the air. "What?"

"We might recreate the scene for old times' sake, except this time we might take things a little further."

"Kael!"

"After all." He grinned. "We *are* married."

"It's not very practical," she began, but before she could

continue her protest, Kael swung her into his arms and started for the honey house.

"That's one thing that's going to change around here," he said. "You've got to start having more fun. You've got someone to share your burdens now, so lighten up."

"Oh, yeah?" She raised an eyebrow, and for the first time since her parents' deaths, she felt young again.

"Yeah."

And that's when Daisy Hightower Carmody knew she had finally hooked herself one honey of a husband.

DEAR READER,

Thank you so much for reading *Kael*. If you enjoyed the book, I would so appreciate a review. You have no idea how much it means to me.

If you'd like to keep up with my latest releases, you can sign up for my newsletter @ https://loriwilde.com/sign-up/.

Please turn the page for an excerpt of the next book in the Texas Rascals series, *Truman*.

To check out my other books, you can visit me on the web @ www.loriwilde.com.

# EXCERPT: TRUMAN

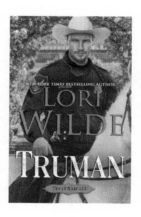

Katie Prentiss was running up the lush pathway of the Rascal Botanical Garden, her ankle-length taffeta bridesmaid's dress swishing between her legs, when a man leaped from behind a maze of shrubbery and lunged for the silk purse clutched loosely in her hands

Startled, Katie swerved to the right but stumbled in her four-inch heels over a bed of pink geraniums lining the sidewalk.

The predator jumped in front of her, barring her way. He wore a ski mask, which struck her as incongruous in the sticky heat. Growling, he snatched for her purse.

Katie's initial response was to flee, but then she reminded herself she wanted to be brave just like the intrepid Tess Dupree, the heroine of her favorite mystery series. Tess wouldn't surrender without a fight. Gritting her teeth, Katie kept a firm grip on the beaded handle.

For one curious moment they stood there in an odd tug-of-war, her delicate, peach-colored purse the coveted prize.

"Give it up, sister," the mugger growled. "I don't want to hurt you."

"Help!" Katie screamed. "Robbery! Purse thief!"

The designer purse had cost her more than her monthly electric bill. Bolstering her courage with thoughts of Tess, Katie refused to let go.

They tussled for a moment. The mugger twisting one way, Katie the other.

"Let go!" the mugger insisted.

"No!" By golly, she would not let this petty thug make off with *her* purse.

A whistle blasted, followed by the echoing ring of metal horseshoes striking pavers. Katie turned her head and spotted a mounted policeman galloping toward them.

"Police! Stop!"

The thief gave a mighty tug, and the purse popped from Katie's hands. The force knocked her backward into the flower bed, her palms stinging from the impact.

He tucked his bounty in the crook of his arm and sprinted for the dense shrubbery like a Super Bowl running-back headed for the end zone.

The officer urged his mount faster. Moving as one, the horse and rider whizzed past Katie in pursuit of their quarry. From her place on the ground, she gaped. The thief hit the thicket inches ahead of the horseman. He wriggled into the underbrush and disappeared from sight.

The policeman reined in his horse and changed direction, forced by thick foliage to go around. Katie struggled to her feet and to her dismay discovered that grass stains and smears of moist black earth marred her bridesmaid dress.

Katie closed her eyes briefly and took a deep breath. She already been running late and at this moment she should be at the Rascal Arboretum, half a mile farther up the road, walking down the aisle in front of her little sister, Jenny. Instead, she stood here dirty, purse-less and feeling rather guilty.

Grimacing, she brushed at the stains. How could she have been so thoughtless? Vehicles occupied all the parking spaces near the arboretum. If she'd been on time, she could have parked closer.

*When will you never learn?* she scolded herself.

She had a bad habit of perpetually running five to ten minutes late. Her father, the psychologist, claimed it was an unconscious act of rebellion, and postulated that the chronically tardy used lateness as a power ploy.

Her mother, the socialite, insisted it was just plain rude. Tess Dupree, Katie's number-one role model, would have been proud. Tess was never one for following rules.

The sound of returning horse's hooves drew her attention. Katie raised her head and caught her breath. The sun, filtering through the park's massive oak and pecan trees, silhouetted the rider in a rosy glow so mystical Katie wondered if the heavens had opened and deposited the mysterious horseman to for rescuing recalcitrant maids of honor.

Goodness!

This guy was even sexier than Tess's husband, Zack. If Tess was the perfect woman, brave, intelligent with moxie to spare, then Zack Dupree was the perfect male—handsome and witty, with a killer grin. Undercover detectives by trade, the fictional Zack and Tess made the ultimate crime-fighting team.

And this cowboy cop, sitting easily astride the tall Appaloosa, reminded Katie of what she imagined Zack looked like.

Then she saw the horseman was empty-handed and her heart dipped to her feet.

"Where's my purse?" she asked him as he reined the horse in beside her.

He shook his head. "He got away."

"How?"

"He had a motorcycle parked on the other side of the hedges."

"Oh, dear." Although she'd been carrying little money, her keys and driver's license were in that purse.

The cowboy swung down from his mount and walked closer. Dressed in black jeans, boots and a black shirt that had *Police* stenciled in white block letters across both front and back. The silver whistle around his neck glinted in the dappled sunlight. A holstered gun hung at his hips. Thick straight hair the color of raw honey was visible beneath a white Stetson. His piercing hazel eyes captured her gaze and held steady.

Katie sucked in air. Something about the man struck her as familiar. Unexpectedly, her stomach fluttered.

"Are you hurt?" he asked, his voice professional yet richly soothing.

"No." She shook her head. "Just disgusted."

"We've had purse snatchers and pickpockets lurking in the park this summer. You shouldn't have resisted him. He could have hurt you."

"I hate being a victim," Katie countered.

"Better to lose a purse than your life. What if the guy had been the violent type?" He took off his Stetson, and recognition crept over Katie. She blinked, unable to believe her eyes.

"Truman West?"

"Yes?" He squinted. "Have we met?"

He didn't remember her. Oddly enough she felt disappointed, although he should have no reason to recall the fumbling fifteen-year-old who had been so desperately infatuated with him back in high school.

As senior class president and championship rodeo bronc rider, he'd never given a second glance to the awkward girl-next-door she'd once been.

Even now, Katie cringed at the memory.

She extended her hand. "It's me—Katie Prentiss. My family lived next door to yours on Lee Street for two years."

"Katie?" An incredulous look crossed his face, then he cracked a smile of recollection. "Little Katie Prentiss?"

"Yes. That's me."

"My." He raked his gaze over the length of her body and smiled his approval. "You used to be so..."

"Fat." Katie finished the sentence for him. She might as well. She knew what he was thinking. As a teenager, she'd been fifty pounds overweight, worn braces and glasses. Nobody had looked at her twice except to snicker behind her back. A fat, four-eyed, metal mouth. Even to this day, ten years later, the taunts still smarted.

"Astounding." Truman continued to stare at her. "Talk about reinventing yourself. I would never have known you."

Katie appreciated his reaction. She'd worked hard to become attractive, exercising an hour every day, watching her diet, wearing contact lenses, dressing in the latest fashions, cutting her hair in the chicest style. She enjoyed stupefying people from the old days. It took the sting out of her ugly-duckling years.

"Thank you."

"Katie Prentiss." He repeated her name again, still shaking his head. "Amazing."

When he smiled, a shiver of delight skipped down her spine. She might have dramatically altered her appearance, but deep inside she was still that nervous fifteen-year-old who'd found all her friends between the pages of books. If it hadn't been for Tess Dupree, the self-confident heroine from an old out-of-print mystery series Katie had adored as a child, she probably wouldn't be able to have a normal conversation with this man.

Truman West was virtually unchanged. He was still the stuff of romantic fantasies. Broad shoulders, narrow hips, muscled biceps—he was any woman's dream lover. Except now, the faint lines at the corners of his eyes, the self-confident aura in his stance told her he'd grown and matured.

"So, what should I do about my purse?"

"I'll file a report for you, but I need to ask a few questions first."

"Actually—" Katie swept a hand at her dress "—I'm sort of late for Jenny's wedding."

"Jenny? Your baby sister's getting married? You've got to be kidding me."

"I know. Hard to believe. But she's twenty-three and her fiancé, Mark, is a great guy." Katie glanced at her watch. "Yikes! I'm ten minutes late already. They must be frantic with worry."

"Where's the ceremony being held?"

"The arboretum."

"That's a long walk. Why don't you let me give you a ride?"

Katie cast a dubious glance at the horse. Ten years ago, she would have given up her favorite books to ride double with Truman West. Her stomach flip-flopped at the prospect of folding her arms around that flat firm abdomen, but the thought of straddling a horse in an ankle-length bridesmaid's gown had her balking.

"It'll be all right," he said. "Tuck your skirt around your legs."

Why not? Tess would go for it in a second.

"Okay," Katie agreed. She would make one heck of an entrance, and the sooner she got there the better.

Truman extended his palm to her.

Katie sucked in her breath and placed her hand in his. She was unprepared for the rush of sensations that swamped her. The memory of her old crush rose to a high flush in her cheeks reminding her of how she had lain on her bed for countless hours staring at the ceiling and pining for his affections.

"Ever been on a horse before?" he asked, leading her around to the left side of the mount.

"Just pony rides when I was a kid."

"Stick your left foot here in the stirrup." Truman placed a restraining hand on the horse's neck. "Grab hold of the saddle horn and swing your right leg over. Don't look so dubious. You can do this."

Katie bunched the skirt of her dress in a fist. *Add wrinkles to the dirt and grass stains,* she thought wryly. Her mother would freak. Hopefully, no one else would notice. All eyes should be on Jenny.

Tentatively, she raised her left foot and slipped it into the metal stirrup. With her free hand she grasped the saddle horn and found herself unable to swing aboard. The horse stepped forward. Katie lost her grip, but her foot stayed firmly wedged in the stirrup.

"Whoa! Whoa!" she said, her voice coming out panicky. She could see herself being dragged through the park.

Truman grabbed the reins and pulled the animal up short. "Calm down. He senses your nervousness."

"This is hard," Katie groused. "You make it look so easy."

"Well." Truman quirked a smile. "That *dress* does get in the way. How about I give you a hand?"

Oh, no! He would touch her again? Before she knew what was happening, Truman bent his knees, positioned his hands around her waist and lifted her into the saddle as if she weighed as much as a baby.

"Up you go."

Truman's voice echoed in her ears and she found herself astride the large horse. Katie felt disoriented and completely out of place, her taffeta dress hiked up to her thighs, the excess material billowing around her waist while she tentatively clutched the saddle horn with both hands.

She turned her head, looked down into Truman's craggy yet handsome face, and the world tilted on its axis. Her breath came quick gasps.

"Scoot forward," he said.

Katie leaned up in the saddle and Truman swung up behind her. His strong arms reached around her, his biceps brushing lightly against her breasts as he collected the reins between his weather-roughened fingers and tugged on them.

He clicked his tongue.

The horse tossed his head and following Truman's command, turned toward the Rascal Arboretum, located deeper inside the desert gardens.

"How are your folks?" she asked, desperate to derail her train of thought. "My mother lost track of your family after your parents got divorced and you moved off to El Paso with your father."

"Dad died seven years ago."

"Oh, Truman, I'm so sorry to hear that. What happened?"

"Someone shot him in the line of duty while trying to arrest a punk kid high on drugs."

"Oh my gosh, how awful." Katie sucked in her breath. She didn't know what to say, and she wondered if his father's death had anything to do with Truman becoming a policeman.

"And your mother?" Katie asked.

"Mom moved to Florida to live with her sister after the divorce. She and I don't speak often."

She heard the animosity in his voice. Did he blame his mother for the divorce? Even after all this time? His pain touched her, and she longed to reach out to him.

Why? Could it be she still carried a torch for the man? But that was nonsense. Her feelings for him had been those of a starry-eyed teenager.

And although Truman had been tolerant of her adolescent crush, he'd never once encouraged her. Besides, he'd dated the homecoming queen, gorgeous Rhonda McKnight. Her gaze strayed to his ring finger, which held the reins, and she noticed it was bare.

Her heart gave a strange little hop at the sight and Katie cleared her throat.

"Did you and Rhonda McKnight ever get married?"

"No." Truman spoke sharply. "Rhonda broke our engagement. She couldn't stand the thought of being a cop's wife. Guess that adage about following in your father's footsteps was true for me. I couldn't imagine myself becoming anything *but* a cop. Especially after Dad died. I felt like I owed it to him."

Katie shouldn't be happy but dam it if she didn't feel a little pleased at the news he and Rhonda had never married. "That's a shame. About you and Rhonda I mean."

"Not really. Rhonda and I were all wrong for each other."

*Darn right,* Katie thought. *You need someone like me. Someone who respects and admires all the hard work that the police do.*

"My work means everything to me," Truman continued. "Everything."

Obviously more than any woman if he was still unmarried at age twenty-nine. And Truman was so fetching in those tight pants and knee-length boots, he probably had to fend off the females with pepper spray.

Pepper spray wouldn't stop the likes of Tess Dupree. Whatever that woman wanted she went after full throttle. Hadn't Zack been a confirmed bachelor before Tess won him over?

Hmm, maybe Katie should take Truman's single status as a challenge. Did she dare?

"So, you've moved back to Rascal?"

"I'm renting an apartment over on First Street."

"No kidding? Alpine Villas?"

"Yeah, how did you know?"

"That's where I live. I'm way at the back."

"Small world."

"It is."

"What about *you*, Katie Prentiss?"

"Me?"

"What do you do for a living?"

Katie wrinkled her nose. She hated to tell him the truth. It was so predictable. Shy bookworm becomes a book-loving librarian. She longed to tell him she was a spy or a private eye or something equally exciting.

"I'm a librarian at the Rascal Public Library."

"You usually did have your nose in a book." He chuckled. "I remember you sitting up in that Chinaberry tree in your parents' backyard reading for hours on end."

Gosh, did she ever sound boring! "I'm considering changing professions," she blurted.

"Oh? To what line of work?"

"I thought I might be good at investigating."

"You mean like a private eye?"

"Yeah. It's silly, I know." Katie twisted her fingers in knots.

"It's not."

"Really?"

"You'd be in for a lot of hard work and it's difficult getting your PI license in Texas, but you could do it if you wanted."

"Oh, I expect hard work," Katie said. "I don't mind that."

"I'm a detective," he said.

"For real? Since when do detectives ride horses?"

"Because I'm a horseman, my supervisor transferred me to the mounted police for a few weeks until we get a handle on these muggings. Normally, I work bunko."

"That's fraud, right?"

He nodded.

"Swindlers, confidence men, Ponzi schemes, things like that," she asked.

"I can see you know your way around the terminology," he said.

"Hey, there have been a few advantages to keeping my nose stuck in a book."

"I imagine that's true. But these days my job is as much tele-marketing and internet scams as anything else. I spend a lot of time online."

"I didn't know the Rascal PD had a whole bunko squad."

"We don't. It's just me."

Truman's chest rocked into her back as they rode. Katie gulped. Was this a dream come true or what? How many nights had she gone to bed hugging her pillow and pretending it was Truman? How many Saturday mornings had she peered from her bedroom window, watching a bare-chested Truman mow his parents' front lawn or wash his four-wheel-drive pickup? Thinking about those long-ago lonely days caused heat to flame on each cheek.

Good thing Truman couldn't see her telltale blush. She'd made a fool of herself over him once; she wasn't about to make the same mistake twice.

"Thanks for the ride," Katie mumbled, not knowing what else to say to the man who had once dominated her teenage fantasies.

"No problem. It's the least I can do since I didn't get your purse back."

Truman's warm breath tickled her cheek, fanning the tendrils of hair that had escaped from her French braid. She couldn't stop herself from sneaking furtive glances at

the corded muscles in his forearms that bunched then relaxed as he guided the horse up a slight incline.

*Heavens, Katie, you've got to stop reacting like this,* she chided herself. But her response seemed beyond her control. No matter how hard she tried, Katie couldn't slow her rapid pulse or stop her legs from quivering. Truman's hot bod tempted her, but it would be senseless to get anything started with him.

*Coward.* She could almost hear Tess Dupree's dare.

But what if she made a move, and he wasn't interested?

*You'll never know unless you try.*

She'd had enough of throwing herself at him and being rebuffed.

*That was years ago. Long before you lost weight and learned how to present yourself.*

Glancing around for something to distract her, Katie noticed that the cactus flowers were in full, glorious bloom. Jenny had picked a beautiful location for her wedding.

Roses of every shade and hue scented the air with their sweet intense aroma. Irises—yellow, white, purple and scarlet— swayed in the breeze. Tulips, daffodils and gladioli reached for the sun. Honeysuckle and wisteria vines twined along elaborate lattices, while delicate posies, forget-me-nots and impatiens flourished in the sheltering shade of willow trees.

They crossed a footbridge. The horse's hooves clopped a steady rhythm matching the heavy pounding in Katie's chest. The setting was strangely surreal, as if she'd entered a fairytale land and was riding through a magical forest with her Prince Charming. Except she wasn't a contender for Snow White, and Truman was simply doing her a favor—but, boy, was she enjoying it while it lasted.

A few minutes later they crested the hill to see the arboretum nestled below. They had transformed a tree-shaded gazebo into an altar with large white wedding bells gracing each corner. They had set padded folding chairs up in uniform rows. Friends and family dressed in brightly colored finery congregated in clumps, obviously at loose ends.

Remorse needled Katie, pricking at her conscience. She held up the wedding and marring what should have been a perfect day for her little sister.

Anxiously, she chewed on her bottom lip but stopped herself before she ruined her makeup job on top of everything else. No matter how hard she tried not to make waves, she seemed to have an uncanny knack for getting into trouble.

As she and Truman rode down the hill, Katie saw her parents break away from the group and walk toward them. Truman reined in the Appaloosa just short of the event seating and the curious guests.

Truman dismounted and Katie sorely missed his reassuring presence behind her. She'd enjoyed being cradled between those fabulous forearms, protected by his broad chest.

Her father's arm latched onto her mother's elbow, while her mother worried her pearl necklace with one hand.

"Katie! What are you doing on that horse?" Grace Prentiss exclaimed, looking horrified.

Truman tipped his Stetson in greeting to her mother and extended a hand to her father. "I'm afraid to report, Mr. and Mrs. Prentiss, that Katie was the victim of a purse snatcher. Unfortunately, I couldn't apprehend the perpetrator."

"Well, I'm glad you were there to take care of our girl, Officer," Dr. Roger Prentiss replied, shaking Truman's hand clearly not recognizing him.

"A mugger! Oh, my! And we just thought she was late as usual. Katie, honey, are you all right?" When her mother worried, she lapsed into the deep Southern drawl of her Georgia girlhood.

"Do we know you?" Her father scrutinized Truman.

"Yes, sir. I used to live next door to you folks. I'm Truman West."

"Why, you are young Truman all grown up, aren't you? It's wonderful to see you." Her mother had to stand on tiptoes to pat his shoulder.

Katie cleared her throat and shifted in the saddle. "Sorry to interrupt the reunion, but could somebody help me down? Please?"

Truman turned to face her. She liked the way he looked, with his mirthful eyes and that irresistible dimple carved in his right cheek. He could smile at her any day of the week.

"My pleasure," he said.

She also liked the way his low voice conjured up images of wet kisses stolen on warm summer nights. Truman reached up and lifted her off the horse.

Katie held her breath against the sensations humming within her body When her feet touched the ground and Truman released her, Katie felt so mixed up she couldn't meet his gaze. To avoid his eyes, she busied herself smoothing wrinkles from her dress.

"What's up?" Jenny asked breathlessly, joining the group.

Grateful for the distraction, Katie turned her attention to her younger sister.

Jenny held the skirt of her wedding gown in both hands and looked radiant despite the concerned frown wrinkling her brow.

"Katie got mugged," her mother said.

"Oh, Katie! Are you all right?"

"I'm fine," Katie groused. "But that stupid purse snatcher got off with my keys, phone and credit cards."

"That reminds me," Truman said, "I need to get your official statement concerning the incident, Katie."

"You remember Truman West, don't you, Jenny?" Katie said. "He rescued me."

Jenny took one look at Truman and her eyes grew wide. "Oh,

yes, who could forget Truman? Katie mooned over you for two years. She'd stare out our bedroom window for hours, waiting for you to come outside so she could drool over you."

"She did, huh?" Truman cut his eyes at Katie.

Embarrassed, Katie grabbed Jenny by the hand. "Mark and the preacher are waiting.

We don't have time to discuss ancient history."

"Yes," Roger Prentiss agreed, attempting to herd everyone in the altar's direction. "Let's get this show on the road."

Jenny balked. "Wait a minute. I want to invite Truman to the reception. Can you come? Or are you still on duty?"

Truman consulted his watch. "I'm off the clock in an hour."

"That's great! The reception's at five at the Rascal Country Club. Feel free to come in your uniform. You can get Katie's statement then."

"An excellent idea," Truman said. "See you all there." He raised a hand, got on his horse and rode back the way they had come.

Leaving Katie not knowing whether she was excited or intimidated.

---

Order your copy of *Truman,* here: https://loriwilde.com/books/865-2/

# EXCERPT: TUCKER

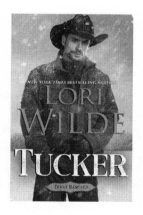

*There he was again.*

July Johnson peered out her second-story kitchen window at the scruffy fellow in a worn leather jacket lounging against her brick apartment building.

Underneath his black cowboy hat, shaggy dark hair six months past the point of needing a trim curled down his collar.

His faded jeans were threadbare; his shabby cowboy boots

were caked with mud, and several days' worth of beard growth ringed his jaw.

He'd been lurking around her small apartment complex in Rascal, Texas, for several days. She spotted him each morning when she woke up, then again before she went to bed at night.

July frowned. Perhaps she should call someone's attention to the situation. Unfortunately, the apartment manager didn't live on-site.

There was sweet Mrs. O'Brien who lived below her, but July didn't want to alarm the elderly lady. And the Kirkwoods, a young married couple, occupied the apartment next to hers, but they both worked early-morning shifts as nurses at the hospital.

Running a hand through her short curls, July considered going downstairs and across the courtyard to knock on the new tenants' door, but something about those two men bothered her.

The Stravanos brothers weren't very approachable. They rarely returned her greetings and never smiled. Often, she'd seen them arguing. They kept late hours and entertained a parade of unsavory characters coming and going at odd times.

Come to think of it, maybe the lurking cowboy was a friend of theirs. He seemed their type—broody, dark, unpleasant. But why hang out in the alleyway? Was he homeless?

July stood on her tiptoes, planted both palms on the counter, and leaned forward for a closer look, her nose pressed flat against the windowpane. Despite his down-on-your-luck appearance, the man was undeniably gorgeous.

The way he carried himself intrigued her. He moved with the controlled grace of an athlete—fluid, confident, unflappable. Heck, he even slouched sexily.

The November wind gusted, swirling debris into the air. The man turned up his collar and his profile. Something about him put July in mind of her favorite country singer, Brad Paisley.

Her heart beat a little faster. Oh, come on, she couldn't be attracted to him, for heaven's sake. He was homeless, or worse...

*July Desiree, you of all people should know you can't make snap judgments. Everyone deserves the benefit of the doubt.*

The cowboy cast furtive glances around the alley, looking first left, then right. Finally, he ambled over to the dumpster that was wedged near the chain-link fence and disappeared from view.

*Hmm, where had he gone?*

Placing one knee on the kitchen counter and boosting herself up, she had to crane her neck at an odd angle to see him.

He looked around again, apparently satisfied no one was watching, then climbed into the dumpster and rummaged inside the garbage bin, giving July a glimpse of his butt.

*My goodness.* July gulped and laid a palm across her chest. *What a glorious tushy.*

He searched for several minutes. Finally, shaking his head, the man straightened, dusted his hands against the seat of his jeans, and climbed out of the dumpster.

What was he looking for? Was the poor cowboy so hungry, he'd been reduced to pillaging for discarded food?

Her heart wrenched, and her natural crusading instincts kicked into overdrive. Nothing captured July's interest quicker than a worthy cause. And this guy had "cause" written all over him in neon letters.

Talk about a diamond in the rough. Despite his disheveled exterior, July saw something special shining through. Shave him, shower him, dress him in new clothing, and July would bet her last nickel he'd make a male version of Eliza Doolittle.

He raised his head and squinted up at her window.

Their eyes met.

Startled, July jumped, lost her balance, and tumbled forward into the sink. Her elbow smacked into the liquid soap dispenser and knocked it to the floor. One leg flailed wildly in the air. Her breast brushed against the water faucet, accidentally turning the handle.

"Oh, oh." She gasped as cold water soaked the front of her sweater.

Teeth chattering, she shut off the faucet and climbed out of the stainless-steel sink. Muttering under her breath, she sopped up spilled soap, then stripped off her sweater and dropped it into the laundry basket outside the kitchen door.

Earlier, before she'd spotted the stranger, she'd been headed down to the laundry room to wash a load of clothes before starting her nine-to-five as a social worker at Hope Springs, an addiction treatment facility. Padding into the bedroom for a clean sweater, July kept thinking about the cowboy.

He had taken her by surprise, catching her watching him. Their gazes had fused, and *whoosh*, for one brief second, they'd forged an instant connection.

A connection so unexpected, it sent her head reeling. Even now, remembering his intense eyes, she felt slightly breathless.

"It's the cold water, you ninny. That's all. Snap out of it."

So why did she hurry back to the kitchen and sidle over to the window again?

*Curiosity*, July assured herself. Nothing more. She wanted to know who this man was and why he was lurking in her alley.

*Curiosity killed the cat, July.*

If she had a dime for every time her family or friends had teased her with that phrase, she would be a wealthy woman.

"Satisfaction brought him back," she said out loud, inching aside the yellow lace

curtains and peeking out.

The alley yawned empty.

The man had vanished.

Disgruntled undercover detective Tucker Haynes swore under his breath and jammed his hands into his jacket pockets.

Hunching his shoulders against the wind and tipping his Stetson down low over his forehead, he stalked down the alley. The trash his targets had thrown away thirty minutes earlier contained absolutely nothing useful to his investigation.

Tucker smelled of garbage, and to top things off, some nosy Rosy in that upstairs apartment had been spying on him.

He'd seen her for just the briefest of moments, but it had been long enough for Tucker to realize he'd been spotted. His impression was of a wide-eyed young woman with a short cap of sandy-brown curls, big green eyes, and a small, pert nose.

Their gazes held for a second, and then she'd disappeared from the window. Had he blown his cover already?

If he had, his boss at the El Paso Police Department, Lieutenant Petruski, would be seriously pissed. Petruski had singled Tucker out for this special undercover assignment that had taken him over two hundred miles outside of El Paso County jurisdiction. It was a hush-hush assignment. Petruski's pet project.

Tucker's mission? Stake out the Stravanos brothers, who were trafficking in counterfeit passports and driver's licenses. They'd been arrested in El Paso but fled after getting released on bail. Petruski had tracked them down to this minuscule apartment complex in Rascal, Texas, but the lieutenant didn't want to bring them in just yet.

Bucking for promotion, Petruski wanted to feather his cap by capturing the head of the operation. He had cherrypicked Tucker for the undercover assignment because Tucker hadn't been involved in the original case, and the Stravanos brothers didn't know him.

Mainly, Tucker's job was to keep tabs on the brothers and provide Petruski with a daily log of their activities. Tucker had been in Rascal for three days, and absolutely nothing had happened.

Well, other than the nosy Rosy spying on him.

Tucker glanced up at her window again, but she wasn't there. He crossed his fingers inside the pocket of his leather jacket.

Maybe she would believe what he wanted her to believe—that he was a homeless man digging for discarded treasures in the dumpster—and go about her business. In the meantime, common sense urged him to get out of the alley.

Tucker rounded the building.

An apartment door slammed.

He stopped cold and pressed his back against the brick wall. Slowly, he inched forward, his ears attuned, muscles tensed.

Angry male voices buzzed in a low hum.

Tucker clenched his jaw and moved closer, straining to hear the conversation.

"That's no excuse," said one of the angry men.

"What do you want me to do about it?" The second speaker had a deeper voice. More gravel and gall.

"He'll be here in three days," said the first man. "We have to be ready. No more excuses; no more bullshit."

"Don't take that tone with me, little brother. You're the one who got us exiled."

*He?*

Tucker curled his hands into fists. Could they be talking about their boss? Was the head of the counterfeit ID crime ring coming to Rascal? Was the ice finally starting to thaw?

He needed to see their faces to gauge what was going on. Tucker kept inching forward until he reached the edge of the building. Steeling himself for flight if he was seen, he quickly poked his head around the corner.

Two men stood arguing in the courtyard thirty feet from where Tucker hid. Big, beefy, ugly. Ruddy complexions, massive hands, and wide feet.

The Stravanos brothers.

The older Stravanos, Leo, waved a burly fist underneath his brother's bulbous nose.

"Don't threaten me," Mikos Stravanos growled.

"It is not a threat, little brother; it is a promise. Get things in shape, or it's your skin."

Tucker smiled. Good. He wanted the brothers at each other's throats.

"Ahem." A gentle hand touched his shoulder. "Excuse me."

Tucker leaped a foot and plastered himself flat against the wall, palms splayed across the cold bricks, his heart galloping.

A petite woman with sandy-brown hair stood in front of him, smiling.

Good gosh almighty, the woman had snuck up on him! What kind of detective was he, letting his concentration slip?

"What do you want, lady?" he growled, struggling to regain his composure.

Her wide green eyes grew even rounder. "Why, to help you, of course."

Help him?

Did she know something about the Stravanos brothers? Surprised, Tucker just kept staring.

"I saw you digging in the dumpster," she explained, sympathy written on her heart-shaped face. "And I wanted you to know that I *understand*."

Ah hell, the nosy Rosy.

"I appreciate your concern." He forced a smile. "But it's completely unnecessary."

He had to get rid of her fast and find out what was going on with the Stravanos brothers. Cocking his head, he listened. They were still arguing about whose fault it was that they'd ended up in Rascal.

"There's nothing to be ashamed of," she continued, her voice soft and gentle.

"You think I'm ashamed?" Tucker shifted his attention back

to her.

"Falling on hard times can be a blow to the ego, but don't let it make you bitter. Anyone can overcome a bad experience. All it takes is one step in the right direction."

"Me? Bitter?" He raised an eyebrow and smirked. Who was this inquisitive little sprite?

A blast of air whipped her hair into a mad tousle, giving her a sexy, wind-blown appearance. The twin hard bumps rising beneath her sweater signaled she was cold.

Tucker had a sudden urge to wrap his arms around those slender shoulders and warm her.

"Everyone needs a helping hand now and then." She gave him a peppy cheerleader smile.

"Excuse me, lady, but what do you want?" he asked, trying his best not to stare point-blank at her chest.

"Would you like to have breakfast with me?" she invited, her grin engulfing her whole face.

"Huh?"

"In my apartment. I'm making steel cut oatmeal and scrambled eggs. You look hungry."

"Lady, I'm a stranger to you."

Her gaze swept his ragged clothes. She pursed her lips.

Plush, lovely lips at that, Tucker noticed.

"We're all brothers in God's eyes," she murmured.

Whew boy, he'd drawn himself a real goody two-shoes. Tucker was just about to tell her to get lost when he heard the Stravanos brothers walking from the courtyard toward the parking lot where he and the girl stood.

He could not afford to get spotted. Suddenly, her invitation seemed like a godsend.

Tucker grabbed her elbow. "Breakfast? Sounds great. Which one is your apartment?" He cast a worried glance over his shoulder, then searched the row of windows above them as he guided her toward the alley.

"We could go through the courtyard," she offered, gesturing in the opposite direction. The direction toward the Stravanos brothers.

"I'd rather go in the way you came out." He tugged her into the alley and breathed a sigh of relief.

"Okay. Follow me." She led him up the back alley.

Edgy, Tucker ran a hand along the back of his neck. He trailed behind her as she climbed the stairs. Her hips swayed enticingly, and he couldn't help noticing how her blue jeans molded to her well-portioned fanny.

*Knock it off, Haynes. This isn't the time or place to get wound up.*

"By the way," she chattered, stopping on the landing and pulling keys from her pocket. "My name's July Johnson, what's yours?"

"Tucker Haynes," he replied before realizing he probably shouldn't have revealed his real name. Too late now.

"Well, Tucker, it's a real pleasure to meet you." She smiled so widely, he wondered if the action hurt her mouth. Looping the key ring around her left index finger, she extended her right hand in a confident gesture of camaraderie.

Caught off guard by her friendliness, he shook her hand.

Her palm was warm and soft.

He noticed that she did not wear a wedding band. His heart lightened while his gut tightened, and he wanted, suddenly, to take care of her.

*How did she do it? he wondered.* Offer a stranger unconditional acceptance? Not smart. But he couldn't let himself be charmed by her guilelessness.

Disguised as a homeless man as he was, Tucker had been on the receiving end of some harsh responses. Most people turned up their noses, refusing him service in restaurants, calling him derogatory names or worse. He didn't expect anything else.

The treatment wasn't much different from what he'd grown

accustomed to as a kid. Tucker, just another punk from the wrong side of the tracks. As a result of the slings and arrows he'd suffered in his childhood, Tucker had trouble taking things at face value. He'd learned the hard way that people could not be trusted.

On the plus side, cynical skepticism served him well in his job.

Apparently, July was one of the lucky few. She had not yet rubbed up against life's ugly lessons.

She was too trusting. No innocent young woman should invite a strange man into her home. Ever. Under any circumstances. And he wouldn't have come up to her apartment if he hadn't been desperate to avoid the Stravanos brothers.

"Here we go," she chirped, opening the door to her apartment and standing aside for him to enter.

Feeling as nervous as a rookie cop policing his first political protest, Tucker walked a few steps into the apartment. His gaze swept the living room, sizing up its occupant in a quick once-over.

The couch was upholstered in a rose tapestry material and adorned with a handmade afghan. Pink, heart-shaped throw pillows decorated the rocking chair. A darker pink floral rug covered the hardwood floor. Figurines lined a glassed-in hutch—kittens, puppies, pigs, elephants, giraffes, lions—a real glass menagerie.

Opposite the window stood a brick fireplace. Thanksgiving decorations adorned the mantel in jubilant fall colors. Orange, brown, yellow, red. Plastic fruit spilled from a horn of plenty. Straw pilgrim dolls sat beside paper turkeys.

Tucker shifted his gaze. He'd never been one for holiday celebrations. To Tucker, the holidays meant only one thing—drunken family brawls that more often than not led to violence, mayhem, and bloodshed.

He batted the thought away and continued his catalog of

July's apartment. A large bookcase housed hundreds of romance novels and a lot of DIY, self-help psychology books.

An ornate Victorian-style lamp sat on a solid oak end table, cream-colored tassels dangling from the shade. Different varieties of dried flowers protruded from various vases placed strategically around the room, and dozens of framed snapshots hung on the walls.

*She has a lot of friends,* he thought, noticing how many different people were featured in the photographs and how happy they all looked.

He thought of his own apartment in El Paso, bare of pictures, and blinked against the sadness moving through him. July's place was cozy, romantic, friendly. The sort of home that made him jittery.

"Come on in. You can hang your hat and coat on the rack," she invited, moving past him into the kitchen. "You can clean up in the bathroom down the hall while I get breakfast started."

Tucker cleared his throat. An incredible awkwardness stole over him. He took off his Stetson and hung it on the peg by the door, but not his jacket. He had his duty weapon in a shoulder holster underneath his coat, and he didn't want her to see it.

On his way to the bathroom to clean the stench of garbage off him, he edged to the window, parted the rose-colored draperies and peered down at the courtyard below.

Dang.

The obstinate Stravanos brothers were still standing by the gate, arguing. Tucker wondered how they ever managed to pull off the complex crimes they'd committed. They didn't seem to be all that bright and fought constantly.

He wished they would move on so that he could escape this place before he overdosed on cheerfulness.

Buy your copy of *Tucker* here: https://loriwilde.com/books/tucker/

# ABOUT THE AUTHOR

Lori Wilde is the New York Times, USA Today and Publishers' Weekly bestselling author of 87 works of romantic fiction. She's a three time Romance Writers' of America RITA finalist and has four times been nominated for Romantic Times Readers' Choice Award. She has won numerous other awards as well.

Her books have been translated into 26 languages, with more than four million copies of her books sold worldwide.

Her breakout novel, *The First Love Cookie Club*, has been optioned for a TV movie.

Lori is a registered nurse with a BSN from Texas Christian University. She holds a certificate in forensics, and is also a certified yoga instructor.

A fifth generation Texan, Lori lives with her husband, Bill, in the Cutting Horse Capital of the World; where they run Epiphany Orchards, a writing/creativity retreat for the care and enrichment of the artistic soul.

ALSO BY LORI WILDE

**Texas Rascals Series**

Keegan

Matt

Nick

Kurt

Tucker

Kael

Truman

Brodie

Dan

Rex

Clay

Jonah

# ACKNOWLEDGMENTS

Cover art by: Lyndsay Lewellen @ https://lyndseylewellen. wordpress.com

Editorial by: Kimberly Dawn @ https://editingbykimberlyd. wixsite.com/home

Proofreading by http://judiciousrevisionsllc.weebly.com